A DEATH IN THE HIGHLANDS

A DEATH IN THE HIGHLANDS

by

Caroline Dunford

Magna Large Print Books
Long Preston, North Yorkshire,
BD23 4ND, England.

British Library Cataloguing in Publication Data.

Dunford, Caroline
    A death in the Highlands.

    A catalogue record of this book is
    available from the British Library

    ISBN   978-0-7505-4234-0

First published in Great Britain in 2013 by Accent Press Limited

Cover illustration by arrangement with Accent Press Ltd.

Published in Large Print 2016 by arrangement with
Accent Press Limited

Magna Large Print is an imprint of Library Magna Books Ltd.

Printed and bound in Great Britain by
T.J. (International) Ltd., Cornwall, PL28 8RW

Chapter One

An Accident Occurs

Under my bed,
Roseleaf Cottage,
Little Crosshore,
X-county

1 August 1910

Euphemia St John,
Stapleford Hall,
The Servants' Quarters,
X-county

Dearest Effy,
(So wrote my little brother in a remarkably fine hand and with a fluidity that I assumed only the boredom of a country cottage could have inspired.)

Thank you so much for the wooden soldiers. I have been having a jolly time with them all day. Mother says you are spoiling me and should have at least waited until my birthday, if not Christmas! Sometimes I think Mother is no fun!

I was delighted by your last letter. You are having the grandest of adventures! Two murders! One arrest! An absconded criminal and so many times when your life and virtue were in danger. Mother nearly fainted when I read your letter to her. The girl-that-does tried to burn chicken feathers under her nose and made such a mess!

I have written to you under your nom de guerre, *so as not to expose your true identity. I'm writing it under the covers to keep it extra secret. Mother said I was to write and thank you for the soldiers, but not to encourage you in your disgraceful escapade. She misses you and hopes you will come home soon. She also told me to say she wonders why you have not written again at length as you did last February. She says you are sending no more than a few lines now and that it can hardly be called a correspondence.*

She gave the money you sent last week to Mr Bulling, the butcher, to whom we owed a great deal. She said he was extremely rude, but now we can have sausages again for tea. Bessy and Tuggy grow bigger by the day, but they aren't yet ready for slaughter. It will be devilish hard to eat them when they are. Why do sausages have to come from pigs? Tuggy is such a little terror. He keeps getting out of his pen and Mother has to chase him around the yard to get him back in. In all those black skirts she is like a giant crow and, as she would say, most undignified.

I miss Pa. So does Mother. Life isn't very fair, is it, Effy?

Anyway have lots of adventures for me and when I'm big and rich I'll buy us all a dozen houses bigger than Stapleford Hall and we will all live happily ever after. Sadly, Mother is still determined I shall go to school rather than letting me start my own business enterprise at once, so it may be a little while until I can afford the houses. Unless, of course, Grandfather ever comes through with the pennies. Mother still writes to him, but he never writes back. If it was Pa he was cross about, you would think he would answer now. If I ever have children I will never cast them off no matter what they do. Well, perhaps not no matter what, I mean there could be dreadful things one might do, but I can't imagine Mother or Pa ever getting up to anything dreadful, can you?

Take care of yourself, Effy. Mr Bertram sounds like a fine chap. Perhaps you should tell him your real identity. He'll get the title when they hang his brother. You mention him so much I was wondering if you might get married? With all that brown hair you're quite pretty for a sister.

Your loving brother,
Little Joe
ps What is virtue? Mother kept going on about it, but when I asked she wouldn't explain.

I tucked the letter into my bodice and sat back on my heels. I had been carrying it around with me for days, reading it often as if Little Joe's words could somehow transport me to a happier place or time. It was a risky action, for the words written within it could expose me utterly.

I had taken a position far below my station and, while the money was most welcome, if any of my employers or co-workers discovered my true identity then for the sake of pride (my mother's) and preserving the societal norm (not that I care of such things), I should be forced, one way or another, to quit my position. This would send my widowed mother, my little brother and me to the brink of destitution once more. We had noble relatives, but for their own reasons they had

11

forsaken us.

I sighed and checked again it was firmly secured. There were reasons I had not again written at length to my mother. These reasons had much to do with the bucket of soapy water at my side and the maid's cap still on my head.

It was 8th August 1910 and much was right with the world. The doomsayers had been forced to hang their heads in shame as the world passed unscathed through the tail of Halley's Comet. King George V was safely installed on his throne. There were rumours that powered flight was only months away from total success and, in the small corner of England where I worked, we were enjoying a most glorious summer.

Of course there were many things wrong with the world. In a less self-absorbed moment I might have mused on the fate of the Russians, that dreadful fire in Hungary or the riots in France, but to be honest I was more concerned with the fourth set of dung-ridden footsteps Miss Richenda has stomped over the marble staircase for me to clean. She had unfortunately large feet and a weighty tread, being one of the more large-boned of the recently ennobled. I remained more than a little persuaded she was attempting to annoy me.

My father is now almost nine months dead and, despite previous hopes of becoming a secretary or more senior member of staff, I remain a maid in service.

Miss Richenda tripped down the stairs again. At least in her mind she doubtlessly believed she was tripping, but it was more of an ungainly lumber. Sadly this thought so unworthy of a vicar's daughter was not one I had the position or right to utter. Instead, quite unfairly, my conscience upbraided me. That Pa should have made such a good job of my schooling and spiritual upbringing is a constant trial to me. In my mother's world, and as she often said: 'Intelligence is about as much use to a girl as a pair of hooves'. Alas, as a maid I also have little use for the brain with which God had in his wisdom gifted me. I am often bored and when so prey to the most unsuitable (if accurate) thoughts about my employers.

'Oh, Euphemia! Silly, silly me! Now you'll have to wash it all over again, won't you?' The eyes that lowered to meet mine did not reflect the smile across her lips. She gave one of her harsh braying laughs, which no doubt her horse would have understood, but I did not. I merely answered with a smile as equally false and a servile nod of the head.

It was small and petty of me to resent her, but it was even smaller and pettier to force a maid to spend the better part of a glorious afternoon in the unseasonably cold marble hallway scrubbing up horse dirt. Yes, I and her younger brother, Mr Bertram, had attempted to have her twin indicted for murder. But the Right Honourable Lord Richard Stapleford was safe at home, having returned from this first sitting as a freshly elected Unionist MP, rather than rotting in jail awaiting execution as, by rights, he should have been. Much it seems can be overlooked for a man with friends in high places.

Miss Richenda continued on her way. In all likelihood she really did want to see her horse

13

again. In lieu of any suitors she was lavishing affection on the beast. That it meant she was able to keep me on my knees was no doubt an enjoyable bonus. She hates me with a passion. She once locked me in a wardrobe, so I am not particularly fond of her either. I slopped more water onto the step and scrubbed vigorously. My long braid swung loose, released by my efforts. My hands were filthy from the job, so I chose not to pin it up once more, but swung it to one side in the hope I could keep it out of the water. I would not be allowed to wash my hair until Tuesday week and I did not want it reeking of horse manure all that time.

My lot was not a happy one. Mr Bertram had managed to preserve my position as a maid at the house. There were things in his father's will that had given him some sway with his brother. He had not been clear on what this was but knowing, yet being unable to prove, Richard had murdered their father put the relationship on the most uneven footing. They circled each other like feral dogs, each unwilling to turn his back on the other. Their metaphorical teeth were on prominent display in what could be mistaken by a stranger for a smile, though I knew each was waiting for the moment to grasp a death grip on the other. But then Stapleford Hall has never been a happy home.

With the departure of their widowed mother to stay with friends in Brighton – can you think of any place less likely to alleviate the spirits? – Miss Richenda had assumed control of the household. This meant she sent many invitations and left all the organisation to the increasingly overworked housekeeper Mrs Wilson. The house-staff had been enlarged to a much more reasonable size, but there was no one else of my organisational ability. I might be paid and named a maid, but in reality I did a great deal more for the household. Especially when the strain proved too much for Mrs Wilson and she had to resort to her 'special medicine'.

I sighed so deeply the letter within my bodice rustled and continued with my allotted task. Water trickled down onto my skirt from the step above. I should not have started from the top. It had seemed the obvious and most efficient way to work, but in practice had created a small waterfall that grew increasingly dirty as Miss Richenda roamed back and forth.

I slopped water onto the step and set to scrubbing. I reminded myself that no skilled maid would have made such a mistake and this was one of the many reasons I could not move on. Despite the abounding enmities within the household I was considered, if not indispensable, annoyingly necessary. Mrs Wilson had even forgotten herself, so far as to murmur what might have been thanks, when I devised a seating plan for one of Lord Richard's highly complex mix of entrepreneurial, minor aristocratic and political guests. Necessity makes the strangest of bedfellows and after the dismal, strange and destructive series of butlers we had experienced, a servant with knowledge of how things should be done had become valuable.

I had heard whispers that a new butler would shortly be appointed and, in a triumph of faith

15

over experience, entertained hopes he might prove to be an ally. I was musing on this when there came a strange cry from above me. It sounded not unlike a pig being led by the ear to slaughter. I looked up as a loud smack followed the cry and I saw the housekeeper, Mrs Wilson, on her way down towards me. Except, instead of using the steps, she appeared to have decided to toboggan down, but without a sledge.

She had slipped on the wet stairs.

'Oh, oh, oh, oh, oh, oh,' she cried. As she passed over each stair her body rose a little in the air, only to fall once more, so her cries of dismay undulated accordingly.

It all happened very quickly, but at the time it seemed to take for ever. I noticed every detail: her pale alarmed face with its tiny beady black eyes widened to almost normal size by the surprise; the thin pink lips parted in an 'O' of horror; her crow-black hair escaping its tightly bound bun and whipping from side to side; her black skirts wrinkling, rustling and beginning to display an old-fashioned set of undergarments as her narrow form bumped over each stair. Most horrific of all was the smacking noise her left arm made as she half-twisted and attempted to stop her fall by holding on to balustrade after balustrade, only to have the soapy water sweep her on.

Without thinking, I moved backwards away from this trundling nightmare. It did not occur to me to stop her. In my defence, I will add that, by the time she was nearing me, she was travelling with significant force. She landed with a final yelp of despair on the black and white tiles. Sadly, these too remained slick with water, so she slid a little more across the hall, slaloming from side to side on the moistened marble, until her head hit my bucket and she was still.

I did not like Mrs Wilson, but this does not excuse my extremely uncharitable reaction. I giggled.

In my further defence I will say she was clearly still breathing and she had been enacting the tyrant over me for eight weary months. I also immediately, or as soon as I got my emotions under control, ran to her assistance. Her thin chest rose and fell in an agitated manner. At my approach her little black eyes snapped open, 'You,' she gasped in tones of loathing. 'I should have known this would be your doing. Help me up at once, girl!'

'Should I not summon assistance?' I queried bending over her. 'You may have unseen injuries.'

She reached up and grabbed my braid. I cried out in pain as she yanked hard with her right hand and sunk the steely fingers of her left into my shoulder as she attempted to right herself.

'Be quiet, girl,' she snarled in my ear. 'You'll have us both over.' A wave of liquor fumes washed over me and I suddenly felt far less guilty about her fall. My hair hurt terribly. I was quite sure she would have it all out by the roots, when her left leg, on which she was attempting to rise, slid from under her, and we both went down in a crashing heap.

Mrs Wilson screamed.

As I lay winded on my back with her spider-like claw still digging painfully into my shoulder, I determined I cared nothing for the bathing rules and I would be washing tonight. My hair, my dress, my skin – all were filthy. For no matter how much I scrubbed, Miss Richenda's constant pacing had ensured a high level of dirt remained in the water.

Mrs Wilson continued to scream.

I realised something must be wrong. I prised her fingers off my shoulder and righted myself. 'What is wrong, Mrs Wilson?' I asked as sympathetically as I could, but at the same time tactically retreating beyond her reach. 'Are you hurt?'

The housekeeper managed to control her cries for a moment. She glared at me, reached out with her hands and, failing to grasp me, gasped, 'My leg, you stupid girl, my leg! Get me out of the hall before the family come.'

'I think it is too late for that,' I answered. My ears detected the sound of heavy, running footsteps.

In a moment a figure emerged through the doorway at the back of the lower hall. My most unreliable and treacherous heart did something odd within my chest. 'Sir,' the words broke from my lips without thought, 'I believed you to still be in London.' Although Mr Bertram Stapleford had been a less than successful champion he had always tried to fight my corner – as Little Joe would say. He was shorter than his brother and, instead of his fierce red hair, had dark locks inherited from his now-absent mother. As was his habit they were oiled and neatly cut. To those who knew him well, his face betrayed his French ancestry as if a subtle veil of difference had been cast

18

over his features, making them finer and more chiselled than his siblings'. He had extraordinarily long and delicate fingers, and totally lacked the bovine bulkiness that the twins shared. While Lord Richard's voice was likely to be sharp with command, Mr Bertram's often warmed with compassion. I could see in his face that already he was empathising with Mrs Wilson's fate. Lord Richard would have already been on his way back to his office writing her an uncharitable dismissal reference after checking the stairs for damage.

'Just back,' he answered briefly as he made to kneel beside the fallen housekeeper.

'Sir, not on the floor!' I cried out in alarm. 'It's filthy!' He ignored me and went down on one knee.

Mrs Wilson struggled to sit, this time sinking her talons into his shoulder and breathing harshly into his face. 'She did it. She!' She flung out an accusatory finger at me. 'She wants me dead, you know.'

Mr Bertram winced at her breath. 'My dear Mrs Wilson. I'm sure this is only some dreadful accident. Euphemia wouldn't hurt a fly.'

I attempted to look demure, pushing to the back of my mind the five flies I had slain earlier in the kitchen as Mrs Deighton had fought valiantly to protect her custard tarts from unwelcome summer intruders.

Mrs Wilson exhaled loudly. Mr Bertram coughed. 'It's not my fault, sir,' slurred Mrs Wilson. 'Since the mistress left and with all those butlers... Mr Harris...'

Mr Bertram shuddered. 'I'd rather not recall

the man. Let's get you up.'

'It's her leg,' I interjected, but Mr Bertram hauled the unresisting housekeeper to her feet. The moment she put weight upon her left leg, her eyes rolled up inside her head and she lost consciousness.

'What has been going on here, Euphemia?' demanded Mr Bertram as he struggled with the ungainly form of Mrs Wilson. I hurried to her other side to assist him.

'Well, sir,' I responded, a mite too harshly, 'being only a maid, I wouldn't be in a position to know the ins and outs of things.'

Mr Bertram had the grace to hang his head for a moment. 'Yes, I'm sorry about that. But as things stand...' He levelled his eyes to meet mine. 'And don't for a moment think, Euphemia, that I don't appreciate that you know everything that goes on in this house. Even Dickie is sharp enough to be wary of your intelligence.'

'Why did he keep me on?' I asked.

'Now is not the time, Euphemia.'

'You say that every time I ask!'

'Good gracious, girl. We need to get this woman to bed and ring for a doctor and you want to stand around here talking about your situation in a manner, I might add, that is quite out of character for a maid.'

'Yes, sir. Sorry, sir.'

'Don't grit your teeth at me, Euphemia. You might try being grateful that you have a job at all. Now help me get Mrs Wilson through to her room. Careful of the floor.'

Grateful! If I hadn't been holding up the housekeeper, I would have boxed his ears and damned the consequences. So really, it was just as well Mrs Wilson was between us. I am not normally this hot-blooded, but Mr Bertram and his often confusing actions do stir my blood. It does not help that he allows me to talk to him in a manner that is quite unfitting for our relationship.

We half-carried, half-dragged the unconscious woman through to her room, which fortunately lies a little beyond the kitchen and not on the upper floor. Despite being thin she proved as awkward in her comatose state as in her waking one. Her rake-like limbs and sagging body required an unusual effort to remove her to her bed. As we finally lowered her down onto the counterpane, I was panting heavily.

'The unconscious are always heavier than the awake,' remarked a red-faced Mr Bertram.

I suspect he felt that, in requesting my help, he had lessened his manly standard in my eyes but, instead of responding reassuringly, I gazed horrified at Mrs Wilson's form.

'Should her leg be bent like that?' I asked. Mrs Wilson's skirts had risen up somewhat exposing one limb lying at a sickening angle.

Mr Bertram averted his face. 'Really, Euphemia. Lower the poor woman's skirts.'

'But I think it's broken.'

'Cover her and I will ring up for the doctor.'

I obeyed his request. 'She was drunk, you know.'

'Euphemia!'

'You smelled the whisky on her breath – sir.'

Mr Bertram sighed. 'It has been a most difficult time for all of us. She was very attached to my

21

late father.'

'Your father,' I repeated in a marked tone.

'Not all children are lucky enough to have as positive a relationship with their father as you obviously enjoyed.'

Immediately I found myself blinking back tears. A stray one escaped onto my lashes. Mr Bertram turned quickly, muttered something that might have been an apology and left.

While he attempted to convince our local doctor to come out to the house I searched Mrs Wilson's room for bottles. I disliked her immensely. She was cruel and capricious, but what Mr Bertram had said made sense. Although I acquitted her of impropriety, she had been most attached to the late master of the house. Now, with him gone and the mistress absent, it must feel as her whole world had turned upside down. Besides I had laughed at her misfortune and, for a vicar's daughter – let alone the granddaughter of an earl (albeit an incognito one) – my behaviour was unacceptable.

I found and removed five bottles; three empty and two whose contents I poured down the kitchen sink. Mrs Deighton shook her head. 'You're a good girl, Euphemia. It's been her weakness many a long year. Considering how she treats you maids. The old master might have turned a blind eye, but I reckons the new Lord Stapleford would have had 'er packing her bags while she was still 'opping.'

'Was she always like this?'

'A drunkard, you mean?'

I grimaced at the distasteful word.

'You know me. I calls a spade as I see it.'

'I know you wouldn't want to see Mrs Wilson turned away without a reference.'

'Hmm, well, that's as maybe, but it goes to my heart to see brandy that good pouring down the drain. A drop of that in this syllabub would go down a treat.'

I stopped pouring, startled. 'I never thought.'

Mrs Deighton shook her head. 'Nope, you started pouring away like one of those temperance people. You're not, are you?'

'Who is going to run the household while she's ill?'

'A broken leg won't stop her giving orders. You wait and see. You girls'll be working harder than ever you have before. Pain is a bad master.'

I stored the last empty bottle in the pantry for cleaning. 'Euphemia,' Mrs Deighton called after me. 'You'd better get a wash before the master sees you. You smell. Sorry, ducks, but I ain't got time to heat you any water.'

I groaned. The only hot water the servants were allowed in this house was heated on the range and, with dinner underway and the master expected home at any moment, this meant a wash in cold water. 'Yer better get that dress into soak too.'

I nodded. 'I'd better stay with Mrs Wilson until the doctor arrives.'

'Doesn't sound like she's going anywhere. Make sure you're changed before the master gets home. He's due.'

My mind suddenly darted back to the hall – the bucket, mop and general mess I had left behind. If I didn't clean it up it would be the first thing the master saw on entering the house. Then I would be the one in need of a reference. I raced back to the hall only to find another set of dirty footprints across the hallway. I could have screamed.

This time working as fast as I could I slopped water around. 'Yer making a right mess of that.' The other senior maid's freckled face, surrounded by its mass of brown curls, bobbed up over the landing railing.

'Merry, give me a hand. The master's due. Find me some rags so I can get this sorted before he arrives, will you?'

'Seeing as you caused the Old Crow's accident, I think I might,' she replied jauntily.

'Merry!' But she was gone. Moments later she reappeared with some rags and together we mopped up the rest of the water on the floor.

'What happened?'

'Mrs Wilson...'

'Nah, not her. The water.'

'Miss Richenda felt the need to visit her horse several times today.'

'Why? Did she kiss it in the hope it would turn into a handsome prince?' Merry giggled irrepressibly at her own joke.

I shrugged.

'She knew you were covering for Daisy's day off, didn't she?' asked Merry shrewdly. 'Cor, but you have a way of getting under people's skin.'

The door behind us opened and in walked Mr Bertram with the doctor. He must have gone to fetch him. Merry quickly bundled the rags into the bucket and picked it up. 'And here's someone what would like to get under your skin.'

'Merry!' I gasped in horror.

'Euphemia!' cried Mr Bertram. 'Why aren't you with Mrs Wilson?'

'I thought I had better ensure no one else suffered a similar accident, sir. When I left Mrs Wilson was asleep. No doubt the pain and shock. I'm sure her leg is broken.'

The doctor, a dour-looking man in his late 50s and a worn tweed suit, unexpectedly smiled at me. 'More like the bottle, if I know Mrs W. Come along with me, young lady, and we can observe the proprieties. You, Bertram, wait outside.'

The doctor's examination of Mrs Wilson was quick but thorough. She groaned when he manipulated her broken leg, but her eyes remained closed. 'Quite right, my dear. A very nasty break. It's a pity you moved her. Was it your idea?'

He fastened a pair of intense hazel eyes on me. 'No, sir,' I stammered.

'Bertram and his desire to have everything in its place, no doubt.'

'I believe he was acting as he thought best, sir.'

The doctor flashed me another curious glance. 'You're a sharp one, young woman, and you're unfortunately pretty. Mr Bertram is the best of them, but don't go springing to his defence too readily.' He tapped the side of his nose. 'Family doctor. You're on his mind and that's dangerous.' He smiled in the face of my obvious shock and patted my shoulder. 'I knew Mrs W when she was young, you know. Used to be a pretty little thing, though you'd not believe it now. I'd rather not see history repeat itself.'

He threw open the door. Mr Bertram shot back

25

into the corridor. 'Going to be a plaster of Paris job, this one. I'll need a couple of men to hold her down while I set the leg. Should probably warn the household there'll be a bit of screaming. I'd rather not give her anything on top of what she's already consumed. This way to the kitchen, isn't it? They'll have the things I need.' And with that the doctor strode out of the room.

I felt my own legs grow rather shaky. I put out a hand to steady myself. 'You've done enough, Euphemia, go and clean yourself,' said Mr Bertram.

'Yes, sir.' I forced my unruly legs to carry me forward. The thought of the poor woman in such pain made me feel nauseous. I took a deep breath and kept my head down. Mr Bertram touched me on the sleeve. 'I'll be down here with the doctor for quite some time.'

'Yes, sir.'

'Down here, with the doctor,' he repeated. I fought the nausea to look up to his face. He wore an expression of exasperation. 'Down here with the doctor, so if some servant should take advantage of my absence to use my bathroom, provided she cleaned up after herself, I would never know.'

'Sir!' I gasped torn between the thought of luxurious hot water and what would happen if I was caught going into his bathroom, which adjoined his bedroom.

'Don't be a prude, Euphemia. It's only a bath for bathing.'

Though I blush to confess it, I did take advantage of his offer and washed as quickly as I could. The bath had a curved standing area with water outlets at one end, so I could eradicate the dirt from all aspects of my person. I have to say, it was quite an amazing contraption, providing what I can only describe as directed indoor warm rain all over my person. I had in the past been tasked to clean this strange new-fangled device, but I had never, of course, seen it in operation. It was quite marvellous.

In very short order I closed Mr Bertram's chamber door behind me and scurried back towards the servants' stair. The hair in my braid was wet, but I no longer smelt of the stable. Unfortunately I had no clean spare uniform and I had not been able to find Merry to borrow one, so I had decided to put on the demure dress I had worn on my arrival. As long as I kept out of the family's way it would not matter. My other uniform which had needed to be washed, after Miss Richenda had 'accidentally' tipped tea all over me, would be dry by tomorrow. Delicious smells floated up from the kitchen. I hoped Mrs Deighton had kept some supper aside for me.

I was almost at the staircase, carrying my dirty garments, when Lord Richard's door flew open and Miss Richenda stormed out. She glared at me and strode past, then called over her shoulder. 'Use Euphemia. She would already seem to be dressed for the position.'

I froze open-mouthed. Lord Richard followed her out. London had not been kind to him. His fiery hair was already thinning at his crown and he had the beginnings of a paunch billowing over his trousers. He stared at me. 'That dog, Bertie,' he barked.

I dropped a quick curtsy and headed towards the stair.

'No, wait,' commanded Lord Richard. 'Me sister may have a point. Why shouldn't you do it?' He came unnecessarily close and tilted my chin, so I was forced to look into his watery blue eyes. 'We both know you're capable of being more than a mere maid.'

I inhaled. He pinched my chin.

'Now, now, I'd rather not hear that impressive scream of yours again. Thanks to my brother we're stuck with each other, Euphemia. I propose to make the best of the situation. You can take Wilson's place.'

'B-b-become housekeeper?' I stammered.

'Ha-ha-ha! Don't worry, it's not for ever. It's the opening of the grouse-shooting season, girl! I need someone to oversee a little hunting party of mine and it seems my sister is not up to the job. I'll take you, Merry and a couple of others, what? There's a local man coming in to cook, Mrs D not being up to the journey. You can oversee the servants for me.'

'Of course, sir. I'd be honoured.' I tried to step back, but he pinched my chin harder.

'Don't worry you'll be well chaperoned, Euphemia. *Up there.*' And then, with blinding quickness, he pressed his bristled lips to mine. The effect was most unpleasant. I pulled back, shrieked, dropped my bundle and fairly flew down the stairs. Behind me I heard his mocking laughter.

Hot tears pricked behind my eyes, blurring my vision, but I refused to shed them. I wiped the back of my hand roughly across my mouth as if my own skin could rid me of his touch. At the bottom of the stairs I paused to compose myself. Why any woman of good breeding should allow herself to be kissed, I have no idea.

I headed through to the kitchen. To my astonishment it was empty. Pots bubbled on the range and wonderful smells wafted from the ovens. The dishes for serving lay, still clean, on the table. Then there came a long drawn-out scream and I realised Mrs Wilson's leg must be being set. No doubt Mrs Deighton had been called upon to chaperone and everyone else not unhappily tasked with holding down the poor woman had made his or her escape. A slight smell of burning issued from the high oven. I looked at it helplessly. Cooking is not an ability I number among my skills.

I stepped into the corridor, only for another scream to send me hurrying back. Nothing connected with Mrs Wilson was ever easy and it seemed it was so with her leg also. The doctor had described it as a bad break. The smell of burning increased. I was almost certain of the oven it was coming from. Taking up an oven cloth, left neatly folded over the back of a chair, I approached the oven door as a cautious trapper might approach a bear's lair. I opened the hatch quickly and pushed the door back. Inside a joint of some indiscernible kind smoked in the darkness. I wrapped the cloth tightly around my hands and pulled out the heavy dish.

'Are you the cook?' asked an unfamiliar male voice.

I whirled round in surprise to be confronted by a tall, well-dressed young man, with burnished gold hair and green eyes of startling luminosity. He was quite the most handsome man I had seen.

Smash!

The dish of meat – never that secure in my cloth-wrapped hands – had fallen from my startled grasp as I turned. The ceramic dish that had contained it, and which I now recognised in the bright light of the sunny kitchen as Mrs Deighton's favourite, split in two and juices from the shoulder of blackened lamb spilt out over the floor.

'Oh!' I cried in dismay. 'Look what I've done.'

'If you don't mind me saying it looks a mite overdone.' There was a faint burr to his accent I couldn't quite place.

'Oh, Mrs Deighton will be so upset,' I cried snatching a plate from the table. 'Maybe I can salvage something!'

'Mrs Deighton? Am I in the wrong place? I thought this was Lord Stapleford's house?'

'She's the cook,' I said kneeling and attempting to extricate the meat from the wreckage.

'Easy now,' said the stranger kneeling down beside me. 'No one is going to want shards of china in their dinner.'

I sat back on my heels. 'It's ruined!' And to my dismay I burst into tears.

'Now, now, lass. Don't fret. It's not the crown jewels. Only a piece of meat. You compose yourself while I get this mess off the floor before someone slips in it.' He gently guided me into a chair and set about stacking the remnants onto a large salver. At the word 'slip' I felt a huge sob rise up within me. Thank goodness I still had hold of the cooking cloth. I hid my head in it and indulged in a bout of hearty weeping for a minute or more. When I resurfaced the man had placed the salver on the table and was running a cloth over the meat juices on the floor by dint of pushing it round with his shoe. This proved to be quite efficient. It was only a pity he was using one of the best linen napkins.

'I'm so sorry, sir,' I said wiping my face clean. 'I'm afraid I've had a rather difficult day. I wouldn't normally indulge in such a display.'

The man stopped and gave me a half smile. 'Would you not? I'm glad to hear it. Don't be worrying if anyone complains – I will take the blame. I should not have been startling you, but I arrived to find the front door open and no one in attendance.'

I blushed. 'I assure you, sir. We are not normally so lax a household, but our housekeeper Mrs Wilson was subject to a bad accident this afternoon and we are without a butler at present, so things are a little out of hand.'

'I see. And who might you be?'

'I'm Euphemia, sir. One of the maids.'

'A maid? If not the cook, I took you for the housekeeper. Although, now I see you without a cloth over your head, I suppose you are a bit young for such a position.'

'Yes, sir.'

'Are you without curiosity? Are you not going to ask me who I am?'

'It's hardly my place to question Lord Richard's

31

guests, sir.'

The man laughed at this, but not in the mocking way Lord Richard would have done. 'You give me too much credit, lass. I'm Rory McLeod.' He held out his hand to me. I regarded him in confusion. 'Your new butler.' he said. 'Never say I wasn't expected?'

'I really have no idea, Mr McLeod.' I said rising a little unsteadily and taking his hand. 'But it is very nice to meet you.'

'Likewise, lass. Now ... this accident?'

I hung my head. 'She slipped on the stairs.'

'And?' asked Mr McLeod. 'There's a bit more to it, if I don't mistake your expression.'

I sighed. 'I'd been cleaning them and she slipped in the soapy water.'

He frowned. 'You were cleaning them in the middle of the day?'

'They were dirty,' I said not wanting to unfold the whole sorry tale and sound like an ungracious servant.

'Hmm,' he said. 'That's not everything, is it? I'm known for my observations. Staff under my care learn this. It's up to them if they learn it the easy or the hard way.'

I bit my lip and wondered what I could say. Another long drawn-out scream punctured the silence. Mr McLeod paled slightly and raised an eyebrow in query. 'Mrs Wilson,' I said. 'She broke her leg.'

'Do you often find yourself in these difficult situations, Euphemia?' asked the new butler.

'All too often, sir,' I answered honestly.

32

'It is the only possible solution,' said Mr Bertram coldly. 'If the party cannot be deferred and Richenda will not go, then Euphemia must take care of the women staff.'

'Oh, you'd like that, wouldn't you?' snapped Miss Richenda. 'Having Euphemia up there with you in the wild of the Highlands.'

Mr McLeod's puzzled eyes travelled from my blushing face to Mr Bertram's furious one.

'Richenda! How dare you!'

We were in the library. The three offspring of the late lord were all seated and Mr McLeod and I were standing. No doubt tempers had been exacerbated by the frugal supper Mrs Deighton had been forced to produce. Although, to give Mr McLeod his credit, he had been as good as his word and taken the blame for the accident.

Richenda poked her tongue out at Bertram. 'Can't you delay it until Wilson is better?' she implored her twin.

'The Glorious Twelfth waits for no man, miss,' said Mr McLeod.

'No, indeed,' barked Lord Richard. 'Well said, McLeod. And neither do the gentlemen I've invited. If you won't come to be my hostess, Richie, then Euphemia it is. Right. Good. Off you go.'

'Actually, sir,' said Rory. 'It's not quite that simple. My understanding of Mrs Wilson's condition is that she won't be able to take up her duties for some time.'

Miss Richenda waved her hand dismissively. 'How long can a broken leg take to heal?'

'Around six months, miss,' answered our new butler.

'Damn it!' cried Richenda. 'Why did the old crow have to go and get herself soused up today!'

'From what I hear if you hadn't been intent on tracking as much dirt through the house as possible to make extra work for Euphemia then none of this would have happened,' countered Mr Bertram angrily.

Oh confound the man! Couldn't he see he was making things worse? I felt Mr McLeod's eyes burning into the back of my head.

'Whatever the situation, I might suggest, ma'am, that for entertaining purposes and anything out of the norm you will require the services of an under-housekeeper for the interim time.'

'Whom did you have in mind?' demanded Richenda, her eyes glittering dangerously.

'As I have only just arrived on staff, ma'am, I really could not say. It would be entirely down to you to suggest,' replied the butler suavely.

Richenda snorted and wrinkled her nose. 'Yes, well, Euphemia had better do it. She's the only one on the staff to have half a brain.'

'Right. Settled. You may go,' said Lord Richard.

'Not quite, sir,' said McLeod. 'With the greatest of respect, there will be the question of increased remuneration for the girl in question. I understand that at present she is employed as a maid only.'

There was a moment's shocked stillness in the room. Then Lord Richard nodded brusquely. 'Quite right. Speak to my man, McLeod. He'll sort it.'

'Thank you, sir. Euphemia?' He gestured for me to precede him and I fairly fled from the

34

room. When we were outside I turned to him and tried to thank him for the increase in my wages. Mr McLeod shook his head at me. 'I pride myself on treating people fairly, Euphemia, and seeing that those in my care are treated right too.'

'Thank you, sir.'

'As under-housekeeper I think in front of the other staff we should use our proper names. Yours is?'

'Euphemia M-St John,' I stammered.

He gave me another of his piercing quizzical looks. 'Between the two of us, Euphemia and Rory are suitable to our stations.'

I smiled. 'Certainly, Rory.'

We were almost at the kitchen. 'It will take me time to come to understand this household. But I will warn you now, Euphemia, I run a very moral household. I will not tolerate liaisons with the family.'

It was on the tip of my tongue to say then he had better tell them that, but I merely nodded. After Mr Bertram's behaviour any protestations on my part would seem disingenuous.

'Well then, lass, you'd better warn your maids and whoever else they're sending up to the hunting lodge they need to start packing. We leave tomorrow morning.'

I looked at him with complete horror. 'Tomorrow morning!'

We were crossing the threshold into the kitchen at this point. 'Aye, the toffs always think packing takes no time at all.'

Mrs Deighton, Merry, the three new maids, the bootboy, two of the footmen and the scullery maid awaited us. Merry grinned expectantly. I noticed her eyes lingering over Rory and felt my spine stiffening. I mentally upbraided myself for uncharitable thoughts. Merry had a very 'warm' nature.

'Right then, ladies and gentlemen,' began Rory. 'I am Rory McLeod, the new butler, and tomorrow I'm taking a pack of you back to my home country for a little shooting.'

'Home country?' asked Merry.

'Scotland, lass. Bonnie Scotland. Your master has bought a new hunting lodge right in time for the grouse season. While Mrs Wilson is indisposed, Miss St John will be acting as under-housekeeper. She will give you instructions for packing.'

And with that he walked off to the pantry leaving me to face a barrage of questions.

Chapter Two

The Lodge on the Moors

Two days later I opened my window to the most magnificent of views. The night of Rory's announcement had been spent in a frenzy of packing. It had taken a great deal of time, not least because I was so unsure of what to ask the others to pack and had doubtless commanded that too much be taken. Mrs Deighton had also taken much comforting.

'What will you do without me?' she had wailed.

'It's because I's too old, isn't it? The next thing you know I'll be turned off without a character.'

'Not at all,' I said knowing I was offering comfort to a woman wholly my senior in wisdom and experience. 'Miss Richenda needs you here. Without Mrs Wilson, the family must depend on you totally.' Probably these demands would not be much more than reminding the new maids to dust and preparing a great deal of cake, but it did calm her.

I, on the other hand, was filled with trepidation. I felt Mr McLeod had tossed a great load on my shoulders, but when I went through to the butler's pantry to demand his assistance I found him deep in the process of cleaning and packing an alarming number of shotguns. I made some feeble excuse for disturbing him and retreated to the comparative safety of the kitchen, where only knives were on display. Which is ridiculous, when you consider the previous deaths at the house.

The train journey yesterday had been long, tiring and dirty. We had arrived late at night and been driven along dark, rumbling tracks in carts so primitive our very bones were bruised by the time we arrived at the new lodge. But this morning, with the cool Scottish air wafting in through my bedroom window scented with pine and heather, I was content.

The term 'lodge' had led me to expect something small and neat. I should have known Lord Richard better. The main building housed the guest bedrooms as well as a dining hall, two drawing rooms, a kitchen Mrs D would have adored, a billiard hall and a library of sorts that was to be used for informal dining and drinks. And everywhere were dotted the skulls of dead deer shot by the previous owners. There was much about the house to admire. It ranged over three levels, with the servants' quarters and stables neatly arranged around a small courtyard. But it was set in the middle of nowhere.

The scenery was breathtaking. We were in the heart of the wilds. Mountains towered above us. A lake as deep as the sea could be seen from the windows and the verdant greenery and abundance made the farmed countryside around Stapleford Hall seem pale and insipid in comparison. I had envisioned a flat moor for the shooting, but looking around me at the rising landscape I could not imagine where the grouse would be shot.

What I did know was it was 10 August. The guests would arrive tomorrow in time for a dinner party, before they breakfasted early on the 12th and went out to slaughter the local avian wildlife. Merry and I had a great deal of dusting ahead of us. For all the talk of needing me to act as under-housekeeper, it appeared my duties were to assign Merry and myself our tasks, oversee the local help who would be coming in to do some heavier cleaning, and liaise between the local chef and Lord Richard. Mr McLeod would oversee the valets, bootboys, stable staff and much of the day-to-day running of the lodge.

I suspect Mr McLeod had taken on more than the normal duties of a butler. I was uncertain if I felt grateful to him for lightening my load, or offended at this highhandedness that had led him to assume I could not manage my new role. To be fair, I was unsure myself if I was up to the task, but I wanted the opportunity to rise to the challenge.

The bell at the servants' entrance rang loudly. I pulled the window almost closed and hurried downstairs. 'Merry!' I called. 'Come on, that'll be the chef!'

Merry had been most wearisomely travel-sick on the journey here. The consequence of this had been when we arrived at the lodge, she was exceedingly hungry. By which point, of course, we were completely out of the wax-paper packs of sandwiches Mrs Deighton had sent with us.

We arrived exhausted at an empty house and we had to make the rooms ready for the gentlemen. There had been no time for Merry to eat. So despite her fatigue and what appeared to be an ingrained fear of the countryside – I could not otherwise account for each jump and yelp she had uttered every time a bush had rustled or leaf dropped into our carriage – I could optimistically predict that the promise of a good breakfast would get my colleague out of bed.

As I hurried down to the door, I put up my hand to straighten the small cap on my head. It felt very odd to be wearing a dress instead of my normal uniform, but I knew it was important that I appeared calm and in control. My father had often spoken of the fiery and difficult nature that accompanied Scottish red hair.

The servants' door was half glass. Through this I could clearly see a slight and girlish figure, not what I had been led to expect by the name Jock Cameron, who late last night Rory had informed me would be our chef. I had been extremely tired by this point and could only conclude that I had misheard. However, as I opened the door there was a distinct smell of cooking bacon and fried eggs. In front of me stood a young woman of perhaps 25 years of age, with long curly dark hair, wrapped in a tartan shawl and wearing a most unfriendly face.

'Hello?' I asked bemused.

'Susan.'

'Susan?' I echoed blankly.

'Aye Susan, your local help. Yous were told I was coming, no?'

I tried to get my head around this tangled syntax and failed. Instead I smiled and opened the door. 'I'm Eu-Miss St John, acting housekeeper.'

'Acting, is it? Can you no do the job for real?' asked the young woman and pushed past me quite rudely. 'I smell Jock has got the breakfast on. I take it there's some for me.' She moved quickly away and into the labyrinth of servants' passageways. I was sure they weren't as complicated as they looked, but I had been too tired last night to learn my way to anywhere other than my bed. I was thus at somewhat of a disadvantage as I trailed after her. The scent of breakfast grew stronger as we walked towards the centre of the house.

Within a few steps we emerged into a kitchen. It was both similar to Mrs Deighton's and yet not. It was large, but not especially bright and it was extremely warm. There was a huge old-fashioned range. To one side stood a great table. George, one of our footmen, was in the process of loading up a tray. A large man, covered from head to foot in chef s whites, towered over the range.

'Any bacon pieces going, Jock?' called Susan. 'I'm gey hungry. I've got the whole of this house to scrub and it'll be much easier on a full stomach.'

The chef turned round, revealing a sun-weathered face, a bushy but trimmed brown beard and friendly brown eyes surrounded by crow's feet. 'Susan!' he bellowed. 'I didnae think you'd be coming back to this place!'

'I've got to eat, Jock.'

'Did you get somewhere local to stay?'

Susan's face darkened. 'Fae now.'

'Good. Good. I'll just load this good man's tray up and then that's the toffs fed. Only the two of 'em so far. I'm about to start the folks' breakfast. There's supposed to be a young lassie of a house-keeper coming to give me orders, but I dinna think she's even out of bed yet! Sassenachs!'

I coughed slightly. 'Actually, Mr Cameron, I'm right here. I'm sorry if you've been waiting on me. I understood Mr McLeod would be giving you the orders for the day until the guests were in residence.'

'Aye. Aye, he did that. But if I'm to go feeding the upstairs I'll need to know how many for break-fast, what sandwiches for the shoot tomorrow, and how big a dinner they expect. It all takes planning, lassie. They grow a fair amount of their own stuff here, but if I'm to be sending for things I'll need to know the noo.'

'I think you will find I have anticipated your needs.' Rory McLeod strode into the kitchen. He was dressed in tweeds and brogues and would

41

have passed easily for a member of the hunting party. 'I've been up inspecting the shoot. There's a few of the pegs have been set up a wee bit close to my way of thinking.'

Jock shrugged. 'I wouldnae ken anything about that.'

Rory pulled out a chair and sat down at the table. 'I'm aware, Jock,' he said softly, 'that there is no love lost between the local people and the new owner, but I will not have either safety or service compromised on my watch. You might want to let your people know.'

The big man shrugged again. 'I dinna ken wha' yer fashing yersel' aboot, mon.'

Rory slammed his palm down hard on the table. I jumped and a small squeak escaped my lips. Rory's eyes flickered to mine, but he continued, 'Ye ken fine. I ken ye've no reason to like the Staplefords, but if ye want yer wages ye'll do yer jobs proper. Do ye understand me?' He paused, took a deep breath and continued in his more usual accent. 'Now if you could see your way clear to serving breakfast. Miss St John looks rather in need.'

Jock grunted. 'She's a peely-wally-looking lass.'

'A bit of respect. This young lady is your housekeeper for the duration of the shoot.'

Rory got up and pulled out a chair for me. 'It's been a while since any man has done that for me,' I said and then bit my tongue.

'Genteel background, is it? Maybe I should convince Lord Richard to retire Mrs Wilson. I don't think he'd take much persuading.'

'Oh, but you couldn't,' I blurted out. 'She'd

42

never get another job.'

'In a fair world we would all get what we deserve,' answered Rory obscurely. 'You! Susan, is it? Come and eat. As I'm sure Miss St John will tell you, after today, we will be expecting a proper early start.' His eyes met mine and I read a reproof. We ate quickly and in silence. When we had finished Susan stacked the dishes. I went to help her, but Rory very slightly shook his head.

'Do you want me to wash these now?' she asked.

'I noticed the last occupants of the lodge have left the front hall less than sparkling,' said Rory.

'Then I think we must make that our priority,' I said quickly. 'As long as you have what you need for now, Jock?'

The chef grunted.

'Right then,' I said trying to sound efficient. 'I'm sure there's a mop and...'

'I know where it's at,' said Susan in a surly tone.

I smiled brightly. 'In that case, you can start by cleaning the hall floor. Merry will join you to dust and brush the stairs. Then we will work up the house.'

'I'll be needing the menus,' broke in Jock.

'I-I ... of course.'

'Miss St John and I need to consult,' said Rory. 'If you've the time, Miss St John, we could go to my pantry now?'

I nodded my assent and tried very hard not to blush.

Rory's pantry was not a large room, but it was commodious enough. Compared to the butler's quarters at Stapleford Hall it was positively luxurious. Having grown up in a vicarage amid the cast-offs from the wealthy, my eye was quick to spot the heavy oak pieces that furnished it were less than new. There was a certain sense of style even if the atmosphere was overly masculine and perforce slightly old-fashioned.

'It's not bad, is it?' said Rory, who seemed to have an uncanny ability to read my thoughts. 'There's a housekeeper's room for you, but I believe it's somewhat floral and cluttered. I doubt it's to your taste but, as Mrs Wilson remains nominally the *in absentia* housekeeper, I'm afraid I can't advise you to change much of it.'

'I wouldn't dream of it!'

'Aye, that's the problem.' Rory indicated I should sit. I sank down in to a green armchair, whose springs gave alarmingly beneath me. I must have looked startled, as Rory grinned at my predicament. 'The thing is, Euphemia, you're gey young to be a housekeeper and the locals here are going to run rings around you. There's no love for the new master.'

'Why is that?'

'Let's just say that our master was rigorous and unscrupulous in putting the estate into what he saw as order.'

I swallowed, remembering Bishop Pagget, who had cast Mother and me out of our home without a second thought once Pa was dead. 'Did you help him do that?'

'Me?' Rory blinked in astonishment. 'What do you think I am? His agent will have done that.'

'And you're happy to work with him knowing what he's done?' The words were no sooner out

44

of my mouth than I realised what I was saying. I blushed fiery-red.

'I'd hazard that you know our master is less than lily-white. I work for him for the same reason you do. Necessity. My father was a grocer. It's a skilled job but, with the march of branded and prepacked food, it's a dying art. I got myself trained as a footman at a big house near here, but there was no opportunity for advancement, so when Lord Richard appeared on the horizon...'

'You jumped at the chance. How did you persuade him?'

'I'm good at what I do. I know the land. And I'm cheaper than a London man. And your reason for working for this unscrupulous, arrogant and mean toff?'

'You were saying I need to be stricter with the servants?'

Rory paused slightly before answering. The long, level look he gave me seemed to say that my abrupt change of subject was crass and beneath his attention. I do not claim to be a thought-reader, and he may have been only thinking of his breakfast, but it was only due to my mother's rigorous training that I did not squirm under his direct gaze.

'Aye. You do. People appreciate knowing where they stand. If you want someone to talk to, come to me, not to Merry. It didn't escape my notice she was still abed.'

'The travelling made her very ill.'

'Can't say I enjoyed it much myself, but I've been up for hours. We need to get some house rules sorted.'

We spent a detailed half hour determining rising times, expected number of guests, when tasks would need completing, orders to be given, our individual responsibilities and finally the menus. It was in this last area that I was able to be of most help. Rory had brought a number of provisions from London, but had little imagination as to how to best use them. I had long done the menus at the vicarage – a combination of Mother wanting me to acknowledge my heritage and start to learn how to run a great house and Pa liking more adventurous dishes. I could no more boil an egg than jump in the air and fly, but I knew to a nicety what should be served with what. My time spent consuming the excellent, though slightly old-fashioned, cooking of Mrs Deighton had also sharpened my sense of what constituted good hospitality. What is more, I knew about game and its hanging requirements. Vicars are often brought such charitable fare and we had a special shed for such offerings at my old home. Little Joe had loved it.

'That's good, Euphemia. You have a knack for this.' He cocked his head on one side and subjected me to intense scrutiny. I smiled back in what I hoped was a frank and open manner. 'You've got some secrets, lass. I can see that. I've no mind to pry but I warn you, if your past impinges on your position, then I will set my mind to discover them. I'm very good at looking into people's hearts and minds. You could say it was a hobby of mine.' It was said with a slight smile, but those ridiculously luminous eyes had something about them that sent shivers down my spine. I had no reason to doubt Rory McLeod, but instinctively I knew he would be a dangerous man to cross. It seemed a good point to bring our discussion to an end.

'I will check on Susan,' I said. 'She should have finished the hall by now and I...'

Rory gave me a direct look. The sunlight broke through the clouds and streamed in through the window. The strange, light colour of his eyes had never looked more intense. 'You do not report to me, Euphemia. We're co-workers.'

'Of course,' I muttered and quickly made my exit. The hall floor was composed of red slate tiles. Presumably because the weather is so inclement in Scotland this was a practical choice. I must confess it reminded me of the inside of a butcher's shop. Susan had made it shine, but not so the grand wooden stair. There was no evidence of the girl and I caught myself tutting my tongue off the back of my teeth, much as Mrs Wilson used to do when Daisy forgot to dust the tops of the hall furniture. It was both unladylike and disconcerting to discover I was prey to such mannerisms. This is the only excuse I can offer for not immediately seeing what was wrong.

'Euphemia!' Mr Bertram hailed me from above. He was leaning over the top of the landing banister and wearing a most unbecoming and uncomfortable-looking green tweed suit. He looked like a man trying to be one with the Scottish countryside and failing. He was as out-of-place as a pair of spats in a coalmine. A slight smile curled my lips and I cast my eyes down quickly so he did not see it. 'How's it going? This

47

place is far larger than I had expected. I hope you have the help you need. I was going to suggest...'
He broke off and I looked up again to see him brushing off his sleeve. 'Good grief, there is something sticky all over this banister. It really will not do, Euphemia. If the locals are giving you trouble, you'd better get Rory to speak to them, or better yet...'

He was continuing with his thoughts on the laziness of the indigenous population when I realised what had happened.

'Bertram,' I shouted. 'Don't come down the stairs. It isn't safe!'

My use of his first name without suffix arrested his attention. 'What the devil do you mean...?'

It gave me the time I needed to run over to the bottom step. Sunlight spilled through the long-paned window behind us clearly showing that several of the higher steps were dull. I ran up the first few shiny stairs and traced a finger along the first dull tread. 'Beeswax,' I said. 'It's not been polished off properly.'

'Good gad!' ejected Bertram. 'I could have fallen and broken my bally neck. Where is the wretched domestic?'

As if conjured from thin air, Susan appeared at the foot of the stairs. She curtsied awkwardly to Mr Bertram. 'I was behind stairs. Someone's moved my cleaning supplies, sir. I was looking for the right cloth.'

'You stupid woman, you left a death trap.'

'I'm sorry, Lord Stapleford,' said Susan.

'Oh, for heaven's sake, get a cloth, Euphemia, so I can get down from here. I don't appreciate

48

having to shout my orders through the whole house.'

'Right away, Mr Bertram,' I said. 'Where are the cloths, Susan? Did you find them?' Mechanically, the girl produced a cloth from behind her back.

'Mr Bertram,' whispered Susan hollowly. The colour had drained from her face. 'Mr Bertram? I thought he was Lord Stapleford.'

'No,' I said whipping the cloth out of her slackened grasp. 'Lord Richard has red hair like you Scots.'

She snatched the cloth back from my hands so quickly it burned hot against my skin. 'I'll do it,' she snapped and scampered up the steps to the first dull tread. I followed. 'At least tell me where the cloths are. It will be quicker with two of us.'

'I said I can manage.'

'What are you up to?' said Mr Bertram. 'Will you get a move on?'

'I didn't know he had a brother,' hissed Susan to me. 'It wasn't my fault,' she called up to Mr Bertram. 'I didn't know yous gentlemen would be down so early.'

'Good gad, woman, it's the country. How long have you worked here?'

'I didn't mean any harm,' protested Susan.

'Will you tell me where there is another cloth?' I repeated quietly and urgently in Susan's ear. 'This is taking too long.' Although to be fair she was working very quickly. However, I could not help be aware of Mr Bertram's fading patience and the growing sullenness of the girl beside me. I foresaw it could not end well.

'If this is the general standard of work...' began Mr Bertram.

The doorbell rang. The chime was so deep I could almost say it tolled. I turned, but Rory was already answering the summons. He glided sedately across the hall, paying no heed to the argument that was brewing behind him. He opened the door to a tall gentleman. It was at this point Susan, instead of fading discreetly into the background, broke into noisy sobs. I immediately attempted to shush her, but she was alarmingly rigid and I had a fear that any moment she would go off into strong hysterics. I glanced up at the new arrival, hoping he would have the breeding not to notice the domestic dispute.

The guest made quite an impression. The gentleman – and he looked every inch a gentleman – had on one of the best-cut suits I have seen in a long time. He had the loose-knit frame of one who was a natural athlete. His hair was lank and blond, slightly longer than is common, especially at the front. I would estimate he was in his fourth decade, around the mid-30s, but there were signs he would not age well. He showed Lord Richard's tendency to run to fat. A fold of skin bulged over his collar and now, as he smiled, I saw a spider's web of lines creased around his eyes. There was also an air about him, hard to put my finger upon, but if forced to name it, I would have said one of nervous excitement. He hid it well, but it showed in the flexing of his fingertips and the manner in which he fairly sprang past Rory into the hall.

'Is this a commotion I see before me?' He

50

brushed past me and was at Susan's side. 'Or is it a flower?' And with that he pulled a flower from behind Susan's ear.

'Oh, bravo,' I said, quite forgetting myself. I heard Mr Bertram mutter, 'Damn it. I'll find another way down,' and he disappeared from above.

'I washed behind my lugs,' stammered Susan.

'I'm sure you did,' said our guest, gallantly presenting the flower to an open-mouthed Susan.

He turned and smiled at me. 'Roland McGillvary,' he said offering me his hand. 'Very popular with young nieces and nephews, available for genteel entertainments!'

I returned his smile and shook his hand. 'Welcome to Stapleford Lodge, sir. I hope your stay is a pleasant one. I am Miss St John, the housekeeper. If there is anything I can do, please do not hesitate to ask. I'm afraid I will have to ask Rory, our butler, to show you to your room. Most of the male servants have been pressed into service marking the shoot. I believe it is quite an extensive area you will be covering.' I was aware of Susan in the background, the flower tucked behind her ear, frantically cleaning the last of the steps.

'Yes, dash it. I'm frightfully sorry I'm early, but I'm such a lousy shot I thought I should take the opportunity to walk the land in daylight before we all start, what?' He laughed loudly.

'It's no trouble at all,' I began, when the front door burst open startling Rory, who had been discreetly waiting in the background, as only a good butler can. Lord Richard burst into the

51

hall. The two men shook hands and clapped each other on the back.

'Rolly, my old school chum! Still making a fortune in chopsticks?'

'Dickie, you old merchant-of-death, you!'

Lord Richard's face suffused with an unattractive plum hue. 'Now, Rolly, old man...'

'Jolly insightful of you to get onto that French gun business. Pity you didn't tip a fellow the wink.'

'Where's your man?'

'Parking the jalopy.'

'Drink?'

It was clear the gentlemen did not need my presence, so only pausing to cast a quick eye over the stairs to ensure Susan had done her job, I signalled to her to leave the hall. Rory had already vanished.

I went through to the kitchen to check that suitable drinks had been laid out in the various parlours upstairs. A very dishevelled-looking footman assured me that Mr McLeod had ensured this had been done before they set out to check the site. He then left, declaring his intention of ridding himself of his mud before dinner, and wearing a decidedly wounded air.

'I'm thinking he's no love of our country,' said the chef, grinning.

'I think you will find he has no love of wearing it,' said Rory from behind me.

I jumped. 'Do you have to move around so silently?'

'Part of the butler training. Now, Euphemia, what was that all about?'

I explained the stair situation. Rory listened frowning. 'You'll need to keep an eye on that,' he said obscurely and headed out.

The next few hours vanished as a thousand and one little tasks and forgotten things made themselves known. There would only be the three gentlemen for dinner tonight but, now it was more than family in residence, I knew Lord Richard would be unprepared to overlook any teething problems.

Once I felt I had the situation under a reasonable semblance of control I retired to the housekeeper's room, with the intention of making a list of what remained outstanding and what could only be done tomorrow. I took out a sheet of writing paper from my desk and stared at it for a few minutes. It was no use. Now I had stopped being busy I could not rid myself of the suspicion that Susan's actions had been deliberate. I could tell Mr Bertram of my suspicions, but I quailed internally at the thought. I did not relish awakening issues from the past, especially as they had concluded so unfortunately. However ... there was nothing for it, I would have to investigate by myself.

By now, I reasoned, the gentlemen would be gathering for dinner and most of the staff caught up with the preparations. It would take only a moment to make my way to Lord Richard's room and check all was in order. Much as I disliked the man, I felt I could not in conscience do otherwise.

However, luck was not on my side. I had just gained the upper landing and was about to open

Lord Richard's door when I heard the sound of footsteps behind me and Rory's voice explaining to the young bootboy when he was allowed on the floor. I darted round the corner only to find myself at a dead end facing a lone door. The footsteps continued. It seemed Rory felt it necessary to show the lad every door. I did the only thing I could and slipped into the room ahead of me, fervently hoping it was unoccupied. Merry and I had been given the layout of the bedrooms, but Rory was charged with allocating them to the guests, so I really had no idea of what I might find within.

In this, luck again was not with me. A portmanteau stood neatly on one side and a fine suit was hung over what I believe is called a gentleman's valet, but denotes a wooden frame rather than a servant. I had entered McGillvary's room. There were no sounds from the adjoining bathroom, so I crossed my fingers and waited for Rory to move on. Shortly afterwards the footsteps did begin to fade and I heard the bootboy's voice, this time repeating nervously the occupants of each room. I was about to make my escape when I caught sight of the book on the bedside table. It was a compendium of conjuring tricks. Without thinking what I was doing I picked up the book and began glancing through it. All I could think was how much Little Joe would enjoy this.

Before I could bring myself to the consideration of the impropriety of my actions there was a noise at the door. I tore my eyes away from the fascinating intricacies of how to make a lady in a palanquin vanish and saw to my horror that the door handle had begun to turn.

Chapter Three

The Nature of Gentlemen

'That'll do, Bobby. If you forget, you come and ask me. I'd rather you did that than I had gentlemen coming to me bootless and angry.'

'Yes, sir.'

'Right, off you go. Supper is due and that looks suspiciously like mud under your fingernails. You'd better get cleaned up before Miss St John sees.'

'Oh, right you are, Mr McLeod.'

The door handle stopped turning and I began to breathe freely once more. I mastered my desire to flee immediately, but I still exited the room all too soon. On my headlong flight towards the kitchen I ran straight into Rory.

'It is not necessary, Euphemia, to attempt to knock me flat on my back to get my attention,' he said, the faint touches of his Scottish burr softening his words. 'Likewise I suspect it is not necessary, nor seemly, for you to appear so flustered. Our guests deserve a calm environment. It appears to me, with the exception of *your* behaviour, all is running well, no?'

'How can you say that?' I answered breathlessly. 'Susan almost caused a serious incident this morning.'

'I think that is open to interpretation,' said

Rory, frowning.

'What else could it be? She hadn't wiped the beeswax off the treads properly and Mr Bertram almost fell. I noticed in time and called to him to stop.'

'People do make mistakes. The last owner said she was an exemplary worker.'

'I have this feeling she doesn't like the Staplefords much.'

'Be very careful, Euphemia. There is enough ill will here without you implying such a serious accusation.'

'But...'

'When I said you should be stricter with the staff I never meant you to forget they are people – hard-working people – and sometimes we all make mistakes. I understand this is new to you and you need to make your authority felt, but accusing the staff of attempted murder is not the right way to go about it.'

'I'm not saying she meant to kill him,' I began.

'Aren't you?'

'I don't think she'd thought it through. And when she learned it was Mr Bertram, not Lord Richard, she was very upset. Ask him, if you want. He'll tell you the same.'

'I am not in the habit of bothering the family with below-stairs issues and I trust neither are you.'

I sighed. 'Look, all I am saying is, I don't think she would have minded if Lord Richard had fallen on his – his ... er...'

'Arse? You may have something there. I'll have a wee word with her myself. As you foiled her terrible scheme,' he grinned, 'she'd be a fool to try anything like it again. I do not believe we have anything to worry about.'

'I hope you're right, Rory.'

'I usually am. And, Euphemia, I won't ask what you were doing up on the gentlemen's floor but, now we have guests in residence, I would strongly suggest you do not go unaccompanied up there again. The nature of gentlemen is not to be taken lightly.'

Hatefully, I felt myself blush from head to toe. I dropped my eyes and said nothing. Rory walked off.

The morning of the 11th dawned grey and drizzling, quite unlike how I understood the month of August to be, but then we were in the wild north and who knew what was normal here? Certainly, no one seemed that put out by the drizzle. The only difference it seemed to make to the local people was the men squashed tweed caps on their heads and the women moved their shawls from around their shoulders to cover their hair. I sat in my parlour going over the menus one last time and attempting not to be dispirited by the patter of rain against the window. In a fit of extravagance I had even asked for a small fire to be lit in the grate and the whispering crackle of the flames was as comforting as the small heat they gave.

My peace was interrupted when my door burst open. Lord Richard, wearing a face like thunder, huffed into the room. 'You'll have to meet me guests. Damned bloody locals.'

I had risen from my desk automatically. 'Of

course, if you think it proper, sir. But wouldn't Mr Bertram...'

'I'll be taking him with me,' growled Lord Richard. 'Try not to offend anyone, girl. Give them my apologies. Tell them I'm dealing with, er, *local issues.* Not that the bastards won't work it out for themselves.' He then went on to employ a very colourful expression on his feelings about being taken for a fool. It is not something I can bring myself to record here.

I hardly knew how to respond to this extraordinary outburst but I did not have to, as yet again Rory came to my rescue. He popped his head around the door and offered to accompany Lord Richard in Mr Bertram's place.

'Won't do, McLeod. Your sway with the locals isn't as strong as you thought. It'll need two pukka gentlemen to sort this out.'

Rory's face closed in upon itself. He replied with a very polite, 'As you wish, sir.' I didn't need to be a mind-reader to know he was seething inside. I tried to catch his eye with a sympathetic glance. Unfortunately Lord Richard noticed and as usual misinterpreted my actions.

'Besides, need someone to keep the wench in order, what!' he barked. 'Has a tendency to go chasing after toffs. I'm relying on you to keep her in order, McLeod. Don't get distracted by those big, seemingly innocent dark eyes. She's as cunning as a vixen,' declared Lord Richard and departed, leaving me gasping for breath at his rudeness.

'That man is insufferable,' I finally managed to say.

'Aye,' said Rory, shortly, and exited. I knew him well enough to understand that to utter a criticism of any kind of his employer was anathema to him. I began to have hope that he would understand the extraordinary nature of the Staplefords. The question was how to encourage such understanding without hastening his departure. Rory might have an unfashionable accent, but he was proving to be an excellent butler and a potential ally among this house of monsters. That he was not unattractive, of course, had no bearing on my desire for him to stay in his post.

The first guest to arrive almost wholly overturned my composure. I was notified in good time of a carriage mounting the driveway and had installed myself at the foot of the stairs. The senior footman had been briefed to meet the valets and drivers at the servants' entrance and Merry had allocated their quarters. Rory opened the door on the first ring and ushered our first guest across to me.

He was a gentleman of medium height, dressed neatly in the first style of fashion, but without ostentation – something that is most difficult to achieve. His dark hair was oiled flat and neat. His complexion was darker than the norm and his rather fine almond-shaped eyes suggested a mixed ancestry. In this age when xenophobia rules I was determined to make him feel welcome. My father had been as clear that all men were brothers as Lord Richard often was on the supremacy of his own race. Needless to say I wholly embrace my father's perspective.

'Welcome to Stapleford Lodge, sir. I am Miss St

John, the housekeeper. Lord Richard sends his regrets but he is unable to meet any of his guests this morning due to local issues that have demanded his attention.' I stressed the word 'any', but I need have had no fears. The guest answered me with the sunniest of smiles.

'I'm afraid I must confess I am not at all sure who is attending this function. I shall be happy to slip in quietly and observe until my company is required. I am Caesar Brutus Smith.'

As Lord Richard had only listed the gentleman as the Honourable Mr Smith I was not, I feel, unjustifiably startled by his name. My reaction must have shown on my face, because yet again Rory stepped in, 'Allow me to show you the way, sir,' he said smoothly and led the startlingly named gentleman up the stairs.

He was barely back before the doorbell rung once more. This time two men burst through the door quite in contrast with Mr Smith's easy entry.

'All I'm saying is the real money is in property,' said the younger of the two. He was a thick-set man obviously set on eating well through his 30s and wearing a sharp but loud suit. 'Whatever is coming, land won't go away. Stapleford has the right idea.'

His older companion also bore the signs of many good dinners in his rotund form. He walked uneasily like a man who fears his skin is about to burst. His hair was short, curled and grey. He smiled a great deal and showed a large quantity of white teeth. 'Now, now, Baggy, let the wisdom of an old man guide you. Whatever happens there's going to be big changes and in all of it there's only one thing you can rely on.'

'Baggy' had at this point reached the stairs and found me in his path. 'What's that?' he said, though whether this was in response to his companion or directed at me, I could not tell.

The older man laughed. 'Man's desire to eradicate his fellows.'

Both men had ignored the taller Rory, who nodded at me over their heads.

'Gentlemen,' I said and launched once more into my introductions.

'Local issues,' said Baggy. 'Is that a euphemism for local girls?'

'I really couldn't say, sir,' I said blushing.

'Leave the poor girl be, Baggy,' said the older man. 'I am Frederick Muller and this is Max Tipton, sometimes known as Baggy.'

'Mr McLeod, our butler, will be delighted to show you to your rooms, sir,' I said quietly. As I stepped back out of harm's reach, Rory took a pace forward, so that we exchanged places as smoothly as the weather figures on a clock.

'Oh pooh!' said Tipton. 'I rather liked the idea of being tucked up by you, me dear. Never mind. Always later – what?' He laughed falsely and brushed against me as he went up the stairs even though there was more than sufficient room to pass. Mr Muller gave me an apologetic smile as he went up, but I could not help but notice his eyes remained cold.

Rory returned fairly swiftly. 'It's shaping up to be gey interesting,' he whispered as he passed me on his way to the door. 'And I don't like interesting. Only one more to go.'

We did not have long to wait. This time a tall, very moderately and neatly dressed gentleman appeared at the door. 'I am William Fitzroy,' he said to Rory – the first man to acknowledge the butler existed.

'McLeod, sir, the butler. At your service,' said Rory obviously pleased. He guided Mr Fitzroy across to me. 'And this is Miss St John, our housekeeper.'

'I am sorry the master of the house is not available to welcome you,' I began.

'I'm not,' said Fitzroy. He had a quiet pleasant voice with a faint suggestion of a West Country accent. 'I'm afraid my valet was struck down by a letter from an ailing mother this morning and I arrive completely unattended, as you see.' He stepped aside and gestured to his bag on the doorstep. 'I would have hated to ask Lord Richard, but do you think I might be able to borrow someone? Not proper valeting, of course. I can pretty well manage for myself, but there are one or two things when a fellow needs a hand.'

Our surprise must have shown in our faces.

'I really do hate to ask, but it was quite unavoidable. I could hardly drag the poor man 500 miles away while she was ailing, could I?'

Lord Richard would, I thought, but I said, 'Of course not, sir. I'm sure Mr McLeod can find someone on the male staff who will be able to assist you.'

'Certainly, sir,' said Rory, though his expression was unconvinced.

I took a short break for a cup of tea in my parlour. I felt rather as I imagine the captain of a ship does when it finally sets sail. Our provisions were on board and our passengers had all presented themselves. I only wished I had a clear idea of the destination of our journey. I felt unease stir my stomach and added more sugar to my tea.

There was a knock on my door shortly followed by Rory entering. 'Do you need me?' I asked rising.

'No, stay where you are.' He sat down opposite me. 'It's me that needs a cup of tea. I have a feeling it's going to be a difficult few days.'

'Why do you say that?' I asked, a little too sharply.

Rory raised an eyebrow quizzically as he accepted a cup of tea from me. 'Was it no you standing with me in the hall just now?'

'Of course it was.'

'I'm speaking about our guests.'

'Well, yes, there does seem an unusual gathering, not to mention having unusual names.'

'To my mind he was the most normal of the lot.'

'What about Mr Fitzroy?'

'He's not a proper gentleman, Euphemia.'

'That's not a nice thing to say,' I said hotly.

Rory held up his hand. 'I meant no disrespect, but you have to learn to differentiate between the toffs if you want to keep this job. Mr Fitzroy is a nice man, no doubt. He's the son of a country vicar – some minor civil servant in the Foreign Office. Couldn't spill his story fast enough to Willie the footman. He's very wary of doing something wrong.'

'Wrong?' I echoed blankly.

'He's not used to mixing with the toffs on this level. Asked Willie to put him in the way of things at the lodge.'

'Oh, poor man,' I said kindly.

Rory winced. 'You're so naive, Euphemia. It's all fine as long as things are going well, but the moment anything goes wrong then it'll all be our fault. It doesn't serve to get too close to the family or their guests.' He gave me a hard look.

I became aware of how interesting the pattern of cracks on the ceiling was and mused aloud, 'I would guess Tipton and Muller are bankers or work in the city? I wouldn't be surprised if Mr McGillvary was in arms dealings. Lord Richard has dealings in all these areas. There has been trouble before.'

Rory did not follow the hare I set. 'You keep evading my questions, but it is apparent you have an unusual relationship with the family. The master appears to loathe you, but yet you are here.'

'I don't think Lord Richard likes anyone very much and I do my job well.'

'According to Susan, you call his brother by his Christian name.'

'What? Oh! That was only because he was about to fall on the stairs,' I said, then added more hotly, 'Has she been implying something?'

Rory took a long sip of tea. 'I think rather than be forced to make assumptions I'd rather you told me what was going on.'

I raised my hands helplessly. 'What do you want to know?'

'Let's start with how the last Lord Stapleford died.'

'He was stabbed,' I said.

'By whom?'

I hesitated only a moment, but it felt like a lifetime. I would have dearly liked to take Rory totally into my confidence but I was aware that my tale was far too fantastic, and explaining the symbiotic relationship that had grown between Mr Bertram and I under the circumstances was as impossible to state as it would be to reveal my true origins. So I offered only the official line, 'By a rogue communist.'

Rory dumped his teacup down on the table. Liquid sloshed into the saucer.

'I know, it's astonishing, isn't it? I don't believe they ever decided if it was a Marxist or a Bolshevik, but then so few people know the difference.'

'And you think I might?' Rory's voice rose alarmingly. A faint flush of anger transfused his cheeks and his luminous eyes glittered harshly.

'Of course not,' I said quickly. 'It was merely a reflection on the constable who conducted the case. I don't believe the truth was revealed.'

'I'll see you at supper,' Rory said abruptly and rose. He was gone before I could ask what I had done to cause such offence.

Supper in the servants' hall was a dismal affair. The local staff heartily disliked their new master and distrusted his servants, while we, in our turn, wished for nothing more than to be home. Rory barely glanced at me. The atmosphere was thick enough with resentment that even one of Jock's sharp knives would not have been able to cut it. I escaped as quickly as I could under the pretence of taking up more brandy to the library. The gentlemen were playing billiards, but might well retire there later. None of the younger servants were allowed to transport hard liquor unaccompanied and Rory made no move to take my place.

I hurried upstairs, clutching my tray. There were no servants' passages on the upper floors, so I needed to move quickly if I didn't want to be caught by any of the guests. I had already began to regret my plan when I heard voices from behind the library door.

Tipton's voice said, 'Look, old bean, I know it's not the done thing to mention this kind of stuff...'

'So don't,' said Lord Richard gruffly.

'But I've bally well put you on the right track, had words in the right ears and generally helped a chap out. It's what one does for the old Alma Mater, what? But it's a two-way street, Dickie. I went out on a limb...'

'Oh stop whining, Baggy, or I'll set the fellows on you!'

'We're not at school any more. You can't just bully a fellow.'

'Be like old times,' said Lord Richard. 'I could do with a laugh.'

'I'm warning you, Dickie, if you try...'

'You're warning me!'

Tipton's voice rose high and wavering, 'All I'll say is influence can turn the tide both ways, Dickie.'

'Why, you little...'

66

There was a sound of scuffling within and a yelping noise, which I presumed to have been uttered by Tipton. I had no desire to rush into a brawl, but I suspected, what Lord Richard could do, albeit unproven, and I doubted Mr Tipton did. Something smashed loudly inside the room. Tentatively, I reached out for the door handle. A hand descended on my shoulder.

I managed not to drop the tray and looked up into the soft brown eyes of Mr Smith. 'I think I should take that in for you,' he said with a slight smile. 'Tipton does tend to bring out the worst in all of us.'

'Then why was he invited?' I asked entirely forgetting it was not my place to ask. 'It seems like a recipe for disaster.'

'Habit, I imagine,' said Mr Smith. 'Whatever his reasons, Dickie's got the old gang together.' I must have looked puzzled, as he continued. 'Dickie, Tipton, McGillvary and I were all at school together. Muller was head boy. Bertie was my fag. Happy days.'

'I don't...'

'No one liked Tipton much then either. He was debagged so often we used to tell him not to bother getting dressed in the morning. Fellows even used to hide his trousers. Never took part myself, but I imagine I'm guilty by association in his mind. But school days are about keeping your head down and keeping in with the sons of your father's friends. That's how the game is played, I'm afraid.'

'Mr Fitzroy?' I asked not wanting to pass up the opportunity for gathering information. I determined the wine at dinner must have loosened his tongue.

'Foreign Office. Dickie's trying to curry favour as usual. Landed a bit of a small fish, if you ask me. Nice enough bloke though. Pretty horrible being among all us lot.' He took the tray from my hands. I beat a hasty retreat. Mr Smith had been nothing but charm itself, but naive though Rory might think me, I knew gentlemen didn't generally gossip with female house servants unless they are interested in becoming much better acquainted.

That night I tossed back and forth in my bed. I had chosen not to use the housekeeper's bedroom and was still sharing a room with Merry. I cannot say if this was because I felt that although I might allowably use her parlour, sleeping in Mrs Wilson's bedchamber was usurping the real housekeeper's status too much, or whether I simply wanted the company. Unfortunately Merry was snoring tonight.

Outside the rain appeared to have ceased, but the wind was whipping through the trees and rattling at the windows. I grew up in the country and the noises of the night rarely discomfort me, but tonight I was prey to grave misgivings. I searched my thoughts and could find no good reason for my fears. I therefore rationalised that I must have forgotten to do something and that it would nag at me until it was done.

I got up and stuffed my feet into my slippers. I had brought a hearty, thick and utterly unbecoming dressing gown with me and I wrapped this tightly around me. In the distance I thought I heard a faint slam. Doubtless I had forgotten to close a shutter. Carefully I lit the candle on my nightstand, shielding the flame with my hand so it did not disturb Merry.

Once I was sure the wick was well alight I stepped out into the corridor. It was very dark and the shadows cast by the single flame danced grotesquely around me. I decided not to take the servants' small confined stone staircase and make use of the main stairs.

This was a mistake. As I stepped onto the main landing, the moon came bright through the long window that illuminated the double height of the staircase. It cast into sharp relief the bone-white skulls of the dead deer that adorned the hall. The shadows of their poor stripped antlers danced like a forest of knives around me as I crept down the stairs still shielding my poor candlelight. At this moment I wanted nothing more than Rory to appear and chastise me back to my room. There was a banging in the distance which grew louder as I descended. I wished I was able to rouse Rory for support, but it was unthinkable for me to approach the men's quarters for anything less than a fire. I could use the dinner gong that stood at the bottom of the stairs, but I could almost hear Rory's soft burr in my ear as he explained that my desire for company in pursuit of a loose shutter would not be deemed a good enough reason to awaken the household.

I reminded myself I had long lived by a graveyard and the dead had never troubled me. Another part of me objected that those dead, as far as we had known, had died of natural causes and not by being hunted and shot to death. Could deer come back as avenging ghosts?

You may appreciate that I was not in the clearest of minds as I followed the increasingly resonant banging through the house. It was with both shock and relief that I found the back door was open. I was relieved there was no preternatural reason for the disturbance, but it could not but occur to me that we might have an intruder on the premises.

I decided not to light a lamp, but to make my way quickly back upstairs. I would awaken Merry and together we would concoct a way of awaking Rory even if it was only to chaperone each other. I pulled the door to and locked it. It was only then that I noticed a faint yellow light cutting across the darkness away to my right, through the maze of passages that led to the kitchen. I had a sudden idea of what might be transpiring. I crept quietly, not towards the kitchen, but to the nearby larder. The door was ajar and, as I looked in holding the candle high above my head, I could clearly see our supplies had been disturbed. But was the intruder still present? It was at this precise moment I became aware of breathing behind me. I grabbed the nearest object that I could use as a weapon.

'Do you think it is quite wise of you to investigate alone?'

The voice was right at my ear. I shrieked and dropped the candle. Mr Fitzroy retrieved it before the light was extinguished and had the pleasure of the sight of me in my very thick, tartan (a nod to our venue) dressing gown with a large dried sausage raised above my head in a threatening manner. The corners of his mouth twitched slightly.

'I assure you, Euphemia, I am not your intruder. I came only in search of warm milk, but I fear my culinary skills are lacking. Perhaps you would be so good as to make me some?'

I lowered my sausage cautiously. 'But the intruder...'

Mr Fitzroy took the sausage from my slackened grasp.

'From the state of your pantry I would conclude they were long gone.' He paused. 'My milk?'

'Of course, sir,' I said shakily. I followed him back through to the kitchen. He sat at the table and observed me. I managed to locate the milk after only two unsuccessful attempts. I filled a small pan and took it across to the range. I let out a sigh of relief when I realised it was still warm. I would have had no idea how to relight it. I was acutely aware of Mr Fitzroy's gaze following me.

'I won't be a moment, sir,' I said.

'There is no rush. It always takes time to accustom oneself to new surroundings or even new tasks.'

My hand shook slightly as I stirred the milk in the pan. He could not possibly know I had never done this before. He saw only a servant – and all servants must be able to do this for themselves. All servants who were raised in the usual way, that is. 'Did you not hear the door banging, sir?' I asked in an attempt to divert his attention.

'I did,' said Mr Fitzroy unexpectedly. 'I was interested to see who would come down to close it.'

I poured hot milk over my fingers as I transferred it to a cup. 'You did not think to do it yourself?' I asked a little too sharply.

'Hardly my place,' said Mr Fitzroy. He rose and came over to me. 'Thank you,' he said, 'I appreciate your efforts, Euphemia, but you need to be more careful.' The dimly lit kitchen was not helping allay my misgivings, but to my ears his tone was quite unlike that of the meek and lost young gentleman who had arrived at our door without a valet.

'Careful, sir?' I asked boldly.

'That you don't scald yourself, my dear.' His fingers brushed mine as he took the cup from my hands. 'I advise you to take more care.'

'What do you mean?' I demanded, but he was already gone into the darkness seemingly needing no light to find his way around an unfamiliar house. I picked up my candle and bolted back to my room. I shoved a chair under the handle of the door, but it was a long time before I fell asleep.

Chapter Four

The Glorious Twelfth

I awoke as a single, tiny shaft of sunlight pierced the thinnest part of the elderly curtains and broke upon my pillow. 'Wouldn't you know it?' I said to Merry as I stretched. 'Fine weather – just as Lord Richard ordered.'

There was no answer. 'C'mon,' I said throwing back the covers. 'We've got work to do.'

It was only when I swung my feet out of bed that I noticed the chair was no longer under the door handle. I rushed to the windows and tore back the curtains. Light flooded the room revealing Merry's empty bed.

After the initial thudding of my heart slowed, I collected my wits and noted there were no signs of violence in the room. Along with her person, Merry's uniform was also missing. I hurried to wash and dress.

The servants' stairs held no fear for me this morning and I quickly made my way along the passages towards the kitchen. A glorious smell of sausages assailed my nostrils. I broke into a run, almost colliding with Susan, who gave me a sneer, a muttered 'Morning' and an unnecessary bang on my elbow as she flounced past.

'Is it breakfast time already?' I asked, horrified, as I ran into the kitchen. Jock was busy at the range and Merry was sitting at the table with a platter of sausages in front of her. She jumped to her feet at my words.

'Och no, hen,' said the chef without turning. 'I'm getting a start on the cold-cooked meats for the shooting picnic.'

'Oh, thank goodness,' I replied. I sank down onto a chair.

'Merry here's doing a wee bit of tasting for me. Maybe you'd like to try a bite yerself?'

Merry flashed me a guilty smile and pushed the plate across. 'I don't think so,' I said coldly. 'There are still the sticks, bags and various accoutrements that need to be sorted for the shooting party.'

Merry bit her lip. 'I've done 'em. I was up early.'

'Good breath of Scottish air just the right thing to set peely-wally young things like yous both right,' said Jock obscurely.

'Thank you, Merry. That was most helpful.' Even to my own ears I sounded stuffy. Gingerly I picked up a hot sausage and nibbled at it. 'Jock, I need to ask you a question.'

'Aye, right, lass,' came the muffled reply from between the pots and pans. 'I really need to start on yon breakfast the noo.'

'I came down last night to find the back door banging in the wind and the pantry door open. Can you explain that?'

There was a loud crash of pans. Jock slammed a dish into one of the upper ovens. 'I'm tae busy thinkin' of naught but the breakfast, hen.'

Merry glanced askance at me. I could feel myself blushing vividly. 'Jock, I need to know if you know anything of this instance.'

The chef turned round. His face was red and sweaty. He was frowning heavily. I had not previously realised how stocky and imposing a man he was. I held my ground.

'And if I won't answer your questions will yer go running to Rory McLeod? Is that it?'

I invoked the spirit of my mother, who in her day did (and I suspect still does) put the fear of God into butchers and bishops alike when her ancestral nature was roused. 'I see no reason why I should go running to anyone, Jock. I am housekeeper here and entitled to know exactly what has been occurring. Although if you do not wish to oblige me I suppose I must ask you to answer directly to Lord Richard.' I bit decidedly into the sausage to emphasise my determination. It was rather hot and I burnt my tongue, but by a supreme effort of will I kept my mouth shut. It worked. My mark hit home.

'Oh, well, there's no need to go bothering the new master.'

'Indeed I hope not. Well?' I raised a single eyebrow. It was a gesture I had seen Mr Bertram use to great effect in our previous adventures. I confess I had practised the action in the mirror, but this was the first occasion I had had to try it out. It worked like a charm.

'Well, now I'm not saying how it was, but it might have been Susan, like. She's gey poor after what's all that's befallen her. The old master never used to mind if the odd bit or piece went missing from the pantry as long as it was nothing serious.'

'And the door? Is it normal practice to leave it unlocked?'

Jock suddenly found his boots of great interest. 'I've a suspicion how if it had been Susan she might have been startled by someone coming down.'

'But someone would have had to have left the door unlocked in the first place. Or indeed have unbolted it after Mr McLeod had made his rounds.'

'Yer dinna understand what it's been like for folks round here!' cried Jock.

I sighed. Who was I to judge one man for taking pity on a hungry woman? 'But it's thievery, Jock,' I said quietly. 'Not to mention the risk of leaving the door open at night for, as you say, such an unpopular master.'

'Susan's no thief!'

'I think Lord Richard would disagree.'

'Yer never going to tell him?' Jock's face was ashen. Merry looked up at me, appealing. I hesitated, but I had better reason than either of them to know how Lord Richard could be when he was crossed.

'No, I'm not.'

'Ah, thank you, hen. It's only a wee bit now and then.'

'No, Jock,' I said forcefully. 'It has to stop.'

'But her wains!'

I shook my head at the unfamiliar word. 'I'm truly sorry for her situation, but I can assure you it will be a great deal worse if Lord Richard suspects what she has been up to. At the very least all of us would lose our situations and, as for Susan, I have no doubt he would press charges.'

'How can you work for sic a man?'

'Exactly the same way you can,' I replied. 'Now, come with me and we'll check to see what exactly has been removed.'

'Do yer want me to make a list?' said the chef from between tightly compressed lips.

'No. I want to ensure that no one other than ourselves realises anything is missing.'

I am sorry to say this was only a partial truth. There was once a time when I would never have dreamed I would allow the ghost of a falsehood to cross my lips, but since working for the Staplefords I have had more than one occasion to wrestle with my innate honesty and – using one of my little brother's colourful metaphors – to wrestle it to the mat and subdue it.

Fortunately, when we inspected the pantry not only were the losses minimal, but it was clear nothing else had been tampered with. Internally I breathed a sigh of relief. The others might see an unhappy, struggling woman in Susan, but I saw the hatred behind her eyes. This is a family prone to murder and, while some might argue that it would only be justice for Lord Richard to be victim of her ire, I firmly believe that vengeance, when it must be taken, is not in the purview of mortal man or woman.

Breakfast passed with alacrity in a flurry of dishes and footmen. The valets and staff attending the shoot ate at much the same time – a highly unusual occurrence that caused Jock much struggling. It was only when all the men were gathering outside that Merry, myself and Jock had the chance to settle down to break our own fast. The local help was not in today. They were either already at the shooting site or had been told to stay away from all the commotion of the Glorious Twelfth.

A dish of Jock's marvellous sausages, a platter of bacon and a quantity of fried eggs lay on the table. It was quite unlike the breakfast we normally received and I believe Merry, as much as I, was eyeing it greedily when Rory strode into the kitchen. His green tweeds brought out the colour of his striking eyes. He wore no cap and the sun glinted off his blond locks. However, his face was thunderous.

'A word, Euphemia.'

I started to my feet. 'I thought you had left!'

'Aye, any moment. If you please,' and he gestured towards the housekeeper's room. Reluctantly, I left my breakfast hoping that either Jock or Merry would think to place it on the range to keep warm.

'I'm not meant to have come out to see the party off, am I?'

Rory opened my door for me. 'Aye, well, sometimes the sight of the housekeeper checking over the dealings for the day is welcome, but no, I don't think it is necessary. It's not as if we have any ladies going.'

'Oh good. I wouldn't want to appear remiss in any attention and show Lord Richard up.'

Rory nodded. 'It's about that I need to speak with you. I've only a minute, so there's no time for debate. If you feel you must come up with the luncheon I insist you keep away from the guests as much as possible.'

'What exactly are you suggesting?'

'I am not suggesting anything, Euphemia. I am advising you for your own good to stay away from the guests.'

'If this has anything to do with...' I began hotly. 'I can assure you there was a very good explanation.' I stumbled over my words as I realised I could not give said explanation.

'I haven't the faintest idea what you are talking about,' snapped Rory. He glared at me. 'If you must know I find myself unaccountably ill at ease

78

around this group of guests. I have a very bad feeling about today. There, mock me all you like.'

I sat down and said in a much more mollified tone. 'Indeed, I won't. I too am suffering from severe misgivings. I need to tell you what...'

He cut me off. 'I don't have time, Euphemia. I have to go. Don't let yourself get caught alone with any of these gentlemen.' The last word was said with unnecessary emphasis.

Seeing that he was genuinely concerned, I merely nodded. I thought everything else could wait. I would wonder over the long months ahead if anything could have been any different if I had spoken then. As it was, I had my chance and did not take it.

In good time for luncheon Merry and I loaded the trap. I decided the best way to fulfil Rory's suggestion was to take her with me to help serve. Merry was naturally delighted at missing a morning's dusting and only too eager to accompany me. Her delight was somewhat tempered as we bounced along the increasingly rough track towards the site. She was decidedly green around the gills by the time we arrived in the little glade that was to host the luncheon.

The bootboy, Bobby, who was also with us, set up the picnic tables and unloaded the hampers. Merry and I quickly set to work to unload the crockery and cutlery. It had been heavily packed in straw and we had to preserve this for the homeward journey. The horse appeared to have other ideas and in the end I suggested to the driver that he take the beast a little distance away, so it would cease attempting to eat the packaging. It was only at this point I noticed the boot-boy too had sloped off. I assumed he had gone to get a better look at the shooting and only hoped he had the sense not to approach in the line of fire.

I was setting the last crystal flute upon the table when I heard the men approaching. There had been no sound of a shot since our arrival for which I was extremely glad. Laying out expensive settings within the sound of gunfire would have been both nerve-wracking and accident-inducing. As it was, I was able to look Lord Richard proudly in the face as he led his little band up to the most elegant of al fresco tables. In actuality the sight was a mite dazzling. The linen was snow-white. The ice-loaded silver champagne buckets glistened and sweated in the heat. The crystal glasses sent sparks of light dancing across the table. The china plates had been polished till they squeaked and the cutlery was the finest the house had to offer. Coupled with the great quantities of food and drink also supplied by the generous Jock I felt there was really no complaint that could be levelled.

Obviously, the killing of hapless birds increases appetite, for the men went through the victuals prepared for them as quickly as a biblical swarm of locusts. I began to fear we had not brought enough when, almost as suddenly as they had begun, the men finished. The dogs scampered around at their feet searching for titbits. I was impressed by how gentle and well-trained they were until I saw Rory call one to heel and realised they were local animals rather than creatures brought up from the south.

The men lolled as much as it was possible in the unsteady chairs – the ground was less than even – and contented themselves with a final drink and a smoke as Merry, the relocated bootboy, the footmen who had been acting as loaders and I began to clear what we could without disturbing the diners. Lord Richard had insisted on using the best of everything and, while we had more of the sets of cutlery and plates at the lodge, many of the serving dishes would be required this evening.

The party showed no signs of returning to the shoot. I paid little attention to them for I was quickly realising some of the plates were far too greasy to repack as they were. I was aware of the bantering nature of their conversation. I cannot say why, but for some reason their jocularity set me on edge. At one point I looked up and caught Mr Bertram's eye. He looked decidedly uncomfortable. Lord Richard's loud blustering tones were interspersed with shouts of laughter. I heard Rory murmur quietly on more than one occasion that time was passing.

'Oh for God's sake, man! Quit nagging!' shouted Lord Richard. 'We've killed plenty of the bloody birds. It's a day for relaxation.' He upended a bottle himself. 'Never tell me we've run out of wine!' He fixed one of our footmen with his beady eye, 'Willie, is there no more?'

I saw Rory ever so slightly shake his head at Willie, who blanched and remained silent.

'Speak up, man!' bellowed Lord Richard.

In the meantime Mr Tipton had risen unnoticed. He tugged at a large hamper on the cart.

81

'Damned heavy, this. I think it's got a little more shampoo in it.'

'Help him, you fool,' barked Lord Richard. Willie threw a helpless glance at Rory and ran over to help Tipton.

The glance did not escape Lord Richard. He gestured for the butler to approach more closely and to bend down close so he could whisper. At this point I noticed that a salad fork was missing. It was only inadvertently that, in my search, I moved close enough to overhear.

'...I am the kind of master you can control,' Lord Richard was hissing, 'you will be making a very great mistake, McLeod. You have no idea who you're dealing with.'

'I assure you, Lord Richard, nothing could be further from...'

'Save it. I know your kind. Bowing, scraping, servile, thieving bastards, who rob us blind as soon as our backs are turned. You need to learn your place, McLeod. You might be a big man to the people round here, but you're no more important to me than...' and he snapped his fingers suddenly before Rory's eyes making him blink in surprise and start back. The table erupted in laughter. Rory straightened. 'I will see to the re-setting of the cooling buckets, sir,' he said levelly. He seemed totally composed, but from my vantage point I could see a faint reddening on the back of his neck.

'Oh lor', Dickie,' said Muller. 'You might want to dally around in the sunshine all day, but I want to damned well kill something.'

'I too have had sufficient,' said Mr Smith

gently. 'It was an excellent repast, Dickie. I fear any more champagne and my eye will be put out.'

'Can't say I mind that,' answered Lord Richard. 'You've been killing far too many of the blasted birds! If I'd realised what a ruddy good shot you were, I'd never have invited you!'

The mood broke and the men laughed. 'Just one more round of shampoo,' pleaded Tipton.

'Oh, let him have his last drink,' said McGillvary. 'It's not like it's going to make any difference to Baggy's shooting!'

There was more laughter. Mr Smith rose. 'I shall return to the site and prepare myself.'

'I'll come with you,' said Fitzroy. He had been so quiet during the meal I had quite forgotten he was there.

A cork popped and Rory appeared with the new bottle. I gazed in dismay at a large dish covered in the melting remains of aspic.

'Miss,' said the bootboy. 'There's a stream nearby. We could wash the worst off.'

I looked down at the boy. He was little more than ten and looking quite contrite. 'Is that where you went earlier, Bobby?'

The boy hung his head. 'I was only having a bit of a scout about, miss. I ain't never been off the Stapleford estate before.'

I smiled slightly, remembering my own child-hood. When I was his age, I had been my mother's despair, climbing trees and building dens. While this poor little mite slaved over his so-called betters' boots and other menial tasks. 'Never mind, Bobby,' I said quietly. 'I won't say anything to Mr

McLeod unless you do. Now show me this stream.'

Bobby grinned and fairly ran off. He led me to a shallow, wide stream, flowing under the shade of trees. The bank was gentle and dry. It was a lovely spot. 'Perfect,' I said. 'Go and fetch Merry and the worst of the dishes.'

It was foolish of me, but this idyll was so like the settings of my childhood that I could not resist sitting down by the bank for a moment to enjoy the beauties of nature. It was at times like this that I realised acutely that I had not been brought up to a life of service and that, by entering it, how very much I had lost. Lord Richard owed me these few snatched moments.

Time passed and my enjoyment of my stolen moments turned to concern. I rose thinking to return to the others when I heard someone approach. I turned, 'Where have you...'

The words died on my lips as I encountered not Merry's friendly face, but that of Max Tipton. Though I am loath to say this of any gentleman, I cannot describe his expression other than as a drunken leer. 'Sir, I am expecting my associates at any moment...'

'Oh come now, my dear. There's no need to be shy. I've heard about you from Rolly. Bertie's gone back to bag a few birds.' He approached closer and I backed away. Within three short steps I found my back against a tree.

'Personally,' said the abhorrent Tipton, 'I've had my fill of bagging feathered birds. Time for me to move on to more lively specimens.'

Damn Lord Richard and his loose accusations!

'Sir, I don't know what Lord Richard has told you, but I am sure you have misinterpreted it.'

'Don't worry. You won't find me any less generous than your Mr Bertram.'

He advanced towards me. I inhaled deeply ready to scream. Mr Tipton regarded my heaving breast in appreciation. 'My God, but you're a bit of special.' He placed his hand upon my waist. I screamed.

My scream was cut off in mid-cry as he placed his large hand across my mouth. 'C'mon, my dear, no need for that.'

I bit him.

He started back. 'You little vixen,' he cried. He shook me off and struck me hard across the face. I fell to the ground, momentarily stunned.

'I think, sir, it is time for you to return to the shoot,' said Rory's voice.

I struggled to my feet. 'Rory. He...' I began.

Rory held up his hand at me. His eyes were locked on Tipton. 'It would be a shame for you to miss the sport, sir. The first flurries have been most encouraging.'

Tipton regarded Rory and something unsaid that I could not decipher passed between the two men. I was reminded of the time my mother's Jack Russell had attempted to face down a fox. Needless to say the dog had been the first to retreat. Tipton shrugged. 'Suppose I should show the others how it's done,' he said. Rory nodded and stepped aside for Tipton to precede him.

I ran up to Rory and clutched at his arm. My only excuse for my behaviour is simply that I was not used to being struck and thus somewhat overwrought. I wasn't prepared for Rory to shrug me off roughly and say, in a voice clearly full of suppressed fury, 'I will speak with you later.'

'But he...' I began and two tears rolled down my face.

It was at this point that our discussion was terminated by the roar of a loud explosion. Both men exchanged very different looks and then set off at full pelt towards the noise. I followed as quickly as I could, hampered by my long skirts.

I was some moments behind them when I broke from the trees into the clearing where luncheon had been held. Merry's prone form first caught my attention. 'She's only fainted. The sound. It was so loud,' said Willie, the footman. I noticed he was pale and shaking. 'I'll look after her.'

'What's happened?' I asked.

'One of the loaders said how there's been an accident, miss.'

'Mr Bertram?' I asked. I didn't wait to hear his answer but rushed down towards the shooting site.

It was closer than I had realised. I almost catapulted myself into the midst of the gory tableau.

I broke past Rory, stopping on the edge of the circle of gentlemen who were crowded around another prone form. At first, I couldn't understand what I was seeing. I took in the man's neatly tailored clothing, but as my eyes swept up his body where his head should be someone had emptied a bucket of raw meat. Bile rose in my throat and the world swayed. 'Oh dear God, that's his head,' I cried.

An arm slipped around my waist steadying me.

'Cover him up, for pity's sake,' said Rory from beside me.

'Who is it?' I asked.

'Smithy,' said Mr Bertram.

Fitzroy broke the stillness and threw his jacket over the shattered head.

'How could it happen?' I asked.

'His gun exploded,' said Bertram shortly.

'Does that happen often?' I asked. By this point I was acutely aware only Mr Bertram and I were speaking. Mr Fitzroy was watching us closely and had thankfully covered the body, but Lord Richard, Tipton, Muller and McGillvary were still frozen in horror. The other loaders had retreated to the treeline muttering and shaking their heads.

'No, by God, it doesn't,' exclaimed Muller suddenly. 'Dickie, who checked these ruddy guns?'

Lord Richard shook himself as if waking from a trance. 'McLeod and myself. There was nothing wrong with any of them.'

'Could it have been an invisible fault in the metalwork?' I heard myself ask. Why couldn't I keep my tongue still?

Bertram looked over at me. 'It's possible, but unlikely.'

'Who was his loader?' asked Fitzroy.

'I was,' said Rory, who had remained at my side. The warmth of his arm around my waist gave me guilty comfort.

'Then you were damned lucky you weren't standing beside him when it went off,' said Mr Bertram. 'Or you'd be lying there too.'

I stifled a small cry.

'Why weren't you there?' asked Fitzroy.

'I was with Euph – Miss St John.'

'How convenient,' said Mr Bertram.

'Leave it, Bertie,' said Tipton awkwardly. 'I was there too.'

'It's a damned rotten show,' said Muller. 'His family will be devastated.'

'Oh God, the Sand Man,' said Tipton. 'He was always deuced good to us as kids.'

Rory removed his arm from my waist and stepped forward. He picked up Mr Smith's cartridge bag and said, 'Gentlemen, may I suggest I arrange for a hurdle to remove the body.'

'Just a minute,' said Mr Fitzroy suddenly.

'Give me that,' said Lord Richard snatching the bag from his hands. 'Don't you touch him.'

'If I might have a look,' said Mr Fitzroy.

Mr Bertram paled. 'Ye gods, Fitzroy, you don't think...' he began and hurried to Mr Fitzroy's side. Together they opened the bag and sorted through the contents.

'Nothing wrong,' said Mr Bertram.

'One more thing,' said Mr Fitzroy. He reached down and checked the dead man's pockets. Mr Fitzroy held up two cartridges. 'Wrong size.'

Bertram fairly snatched these out of his hands. 'Damn it, you're right. It's murder,' said Mr Bertram.

Like a hungry pack of wolves scenting prey, all the men turned their eyes to Rory.

Chapter Five

The Butler Did It

As one, the gentlemen moved towards Rory. The butler took a step back then held his ground. He raised his hands in the air in a gesture of surrender. 'I assure you, gentlemen, I had nothing to do with this.'

'Get him!' yelled Lord Richard. There was an unseemly scuffle during which Rory offered no resistance to a rough and amateur subduing. I have no doubt if he had chosen he could have thrown his assailants to the ground, but he didn't. Moments later, sweating from their unnecessary and brutish effort, Tipton and McGillvary were grinning in victory as they pinned Rory's arms behind his back.

'But it makes no sense,' I cried. 'Why would Rory harm Mr Smith?'

'What's happened?' Merry's quavering voice came from behind me. For reasons that only Willie could fathom he had brought her down to the site. Perhaps he wished to help, but bringing Merry with him was decidedly a bad idea.

'Will someone get these bloody women out of the way?' blustered Lord Richard. 'McLeod – no, not you, obviously,' he stopped confused.

'But what do we do?' asked Tipton hopelessly.

'Like the man said we need to get a hurdle from

the house,' said Lord Richard. 'You, Willie, see to it.'

'Shouldn't we summon the police?' said Mr Bertram.

'Damn it. We can't leave the man lying on the ground.'

'But you'll disturb the crime scene,' I said.

Fitzroy gave me an odd look. Everyone else ignored me. 'I suggest I return with the women to the house,' he said quietly. 'If I use my contacts at the Department I should be able to get us someone discreet.'

'Good thinking, Fitzroy,' said Lord Richard. 'The last thing we want is the local plod stomping round here.'

'Euphemia has a point about not moving the body,' said Mr Bertram, who apparently had heard me after all.

'Indeed,' said Fitzroy, 'but I am very much afraid that an inspector of the kind we require is unlikely to be local and thus even more unlikely to be with us today.'

The others looked at him blankly. 'So?' said Mr Bertram.

'Foxes,' said Fitzroy casting a glance at the very pale Merry.

'Oh gad! You mean...' said Tipton. He plastered his hand to his mouth and then ran from the scene.

Merry looked at me for explanation. I said nothing. Unfortunately Lord Richard did. 'Yes, by God, can't leave the man's brains as an entrée for the local wildlife.' He stopped at the sound of a thump and swung round. 'What?' Merry had swooned to the ground. 'Will someone get these damned women out of here!'

'As I said,' said Fitzroy in a firmer voice, 'I would be happy to escort the housekeeper and her assistant back to the house. If Willie will come with us we can arrange for a hurdle to be sent back. I will summon the police from the house.'

'Dammit, I'm coming with you,' said Muller. 'I'm not staying here with that.'

'I regret that with the women, McLeod, Willie and myself there will be no more room,' said Fitzroy smoothly. 'If I might suggest most of you retire to the clearing? I can summon the police from the house phone. If this would be agreeable to you, Lord Richard.'

'Fine,' said Lord Richard. 'I need a drink.' He stalked off in the direction of the clearing.

'I'll stay with the corpse,' said Mr Bertram.

Mr Fitzroy nodded. He approached Rory, who was still being held by McGillvary. 'I am sure we could find rope to bind you,' he said, 'but if you will give me your word you will not try to escape I do not think it will be necessary.'

'Good gad! You can't expect this murdering bast ... er, bounder to simply sit in the carriage,' said Mr Bertram.

'I will take a gun,' said Fitzroy.

'There will be no need,' said Rory gruffly. 'I did not kill this man.'

Fitzroy smiled. 'Innocence is the second-best defence,' he said obscurely.

The journey back was extremely unpleasant. Rory kept his face averted from me. Willie didn't know where to look as he sat next to the man who, only moments before, had been the subject of his admiration. Merry kept the edge of her apron pressed to her mouth. Her eyes flickered from side to side as the combination of natural horror and her travel-sick stomach constantly threatened to overwhelm her. Fitzroy was the only one of us to seem relaxed. He sat with the gun across his knee as if it were the most natural accessory to a gentleman's costume. I remembered Rory had said Fitzroy had come from humble country gentry. My thoughts whirled around my head as busy as a hive of angry bees.

As I alighted at the lodge I drew Mr Fitzroy to one side. 'Sir, I cannot believe this of Mr McLeod. I...'

'I do not believe at this time you can have more information to offer unless McLeod has confessed to you. Has he?'

'No, he has not!'

'Then, if you will not think it impertinent of me, I will suggest that you see to taking up the reins of Lord Richard's staff. The house is bound to be in chaos for some time, but I have often remarked how the orderly presentation of meals and preservation of the semblance of manners help smooth things quickly towards a natural conclusion, even in a place as isolated from city living as this.'

His voice was back to its previous soft and smooth tones, but I read a warning in his eyes. 'Hunting can put up the blood of even the most civilised man.'

The memory of how the men had leapt upon

Rory as the murderer was fresh in my mind. I felt myself grow a little dizzy. 'You mean the men might decide to take the law into their own hands?'

'I would never suggest a gentleman would forget his honour, but in cases such as this, emotion can overshadow reason.'

'You don't think he did it either!' I cried.

'I think, for all our sakes, you must secure Mr Rory McLeod in a room to which only you hold the key and as quickly as possible.'

'Of course,' I said. 'Willie! Rory! This way!'

I fairly bustled them through the hall, but not before I had occasion to hear Fitzroy say into the telephone in strangely clipped and terse accents, 'Fitzroy. I need Edward. It's happened.'

I chose the second pantry as the site for Rory's incarceration. It was far enough removed from the general servants' quarters that no one should have reason for hanging around in the area. He would be left alone. It was empty and of a size to have a truckle bed erected easily. I had Willie do this and provide the necessary amenities. I attempted to ask Rory if there was anything else I could do for him, but he turned his face to the wall.

'I do understand your pride must be sorely hurt, Rory, but until this matter is suitably resolved can you not be pleased that it is I that have the charge of you, rather than Lord Richard?'

'I'm meant to feel grateful, am I?' Rory spoke to the wall.

'No, I didn't mean that.'

'Go away, Euphemia. You're going to be busy.'

I sighed and left, locking the door carefully behind me. Rory had spoken no less than the truth. The rest of the day dissolved into such turmoil that I was sure it would remain in my nightmares for the rest of my life. The men returned and, contrary to my expectations, made a good meal of the tea I had hurriedly laid out for them. They then retired to drink whisky and talk very loudly.

There was a great deal of unfortunate discussion as to where to place Mr Smith's body. Lord Richard would not have it in the upper house and I stood my ground declaring it was unsanitary and could not be put safely near either the kitchen or the servants' sleeping quarters. In the end, the poor man was stabled in an outside shed and the gardener was paid five shillings to stand over the body with a gun to prevent any assault by wildlife.

When I finally fell into my bed that night, my body was numb with fatigue but my brain still reeled with the implications of it all. Fitzroy was right – I did not have enough information to understand what had occurred, but I could not believe Rory capable of murder. I finally fell asleep to the sound of Merry sobbing. I had not realised she liked Rory quite so much.

The bright light of dawn brought little comfort. I chased the servants into order. Although violent murder is naturally disturbing, having lived through the experience twice before, I knew it was possible to move through this time of chaos to a calmer place. I decided not to share my experiences with our newer servants as it might give them a false impression of our household. I might also add that, as a vicar's daughter, I had on many occasions dealt with the business of natural death. I had no terror of the grave as it seemed many of our suspicious Scottish servants did. I was neither impressed nor surprised when many of the local help did not arrive in the morning. I put Merry to extra duties as I felt sure the activity would lessen her preoccupation with our circumstances. The natural annoyance with which she greeted my dictates suggested I was correct.

The doorbell rang sharply three times before it struck me there was no Rory to open it and I hurried to do the task myself. On the threshold stood a man of middle years in a distinguished brown suit with a generally mild and unprepossessing face that was only lent any distinction by a pair of extremely bushy eyebrows.

'I am Mr Edward,' he said in a strong, authoritarian voice. 'I am here to investigate the murder.'

He held up a little wallet with some insignia on it. It meant nothing to me.

'I would like to see Lord Richard immediately.'

'He is at breakfast, sir,' I said. 'I can show you to a room where you can wait. Would you like some refreshment? Perhaps coffee?'

The eyebrows descended into a ferocious frown the like of which I have rarely seen. 'And you are?'

'Miss St John, the housekeeper.'

'Well, Miss St John, I said I need to see the master of the house now and I meant *now.*'

There was a clatter of footsteps on the stair

behind me. 'Hullo!' called Mr Bertram. 'I'm his brother. Can I be of assistance? Miss St John is quite correct – my brother left strict orders not to be disturbed at breakfast. He can be a bit of a bear in the morning.'

'I am here, sir, to investigate a murder. I hope I can assume that, in any good Christian household, the subject of unlawful killing would take precedence over morning rolls.'

'Of course,' said Mr Bertram. He reached my side and opened the door wider. I knew him well enough to know our visitor was disconcerting him. 'You're from?'

Mr Edward thrust the little wallet at him. It may have been my imagination, but Mr Bertram went a little paler.

'I understand the wrong cartridge was put in the man's bag. Why did you have them on the premises?' asked Mr Edward.

My imagination does like to play tricks on me, but as Mr Edward stepped into the hall he seemed to grow larger and it smaller.

'I couldn't really say,' said Mr Bertram. 'No wait. At one point my sister was considering attending and she would have used a smaller gun.'

'She shoots?'

'Not awfully well,' said Mr Bertram with an attempt at a laugh.

'And she withdrew from the party? Why?'

'I don't think she ever fancied attending much,' said Mr Bertram. 'My brother wanted a hostess. Our housekeeper had broken her leg and was unable to attend.'

Mr Edward looked me up and down. 'A remarkable recovery?' he asked.

'He means Mrs Wilson, sir,' I interposed.

'What happened to her?'

'She slipped on some stairs I had been cleaning,' I said quickly. 'It was an accident.'

'So you were promoted?' said Mr Edward.

'*Temporarily*, sir,' I said stressing the first word.

'Come in, sir. I'm sure my brother will be happy – well, not happy under the circumstances, but relieved to see you. Hopefully this will all turn out to be some terrible mistake.'

'You don't believe the butler did it?'

'I can't for the life of me see why he would. If this isn't a dreadful accident – and I'm hoping to God it is – then it would have to be a politically motivated murder,' said Mr Bertram to my astonishment.

'It's very interesting to hear you say so, sir,' said Mr Edward. 'Were you aware your butler is a member of the Communist Party?'

Mr Bertram froze. 'No, I was not,' he said in a strained voice.

'Your family has previously been the victim of a Bolshevik plot, have they not?'

'The matter was never formally resolved,' said Mr Bertram quietly. 'If you could come this way.'

The two men moved off leaving me by the open door. It was some few minutes before I could collect my wits and shut it. I wandered back to the kitchen in a daze. Could I have been wrong about Rory? There had to be another explanation.

The kitchen was a hive of activity. The breakfast dishes had been sent down and, at my instruction, Jock was preparing a lunch that could be served both upstairs and outside, if the gentlemen decided to leave the house.

Merry, her cap rather fetchingly askew, rushed over to me. 'I can't manage,' she said. 'I've done no dusting, the beds need done and now Jock tells me I have to wash the breakfast crockery. It's not possible, Euphemia.'

'Where's Susan?' I asked.

'Not here,' rumbled Jock. I gave him a look I had learnt from my mother. 'Aye, I know, lass. After you giving her another chance and all. I thought when I talked to her we'd got it all straightened. I never...'

'I'm going out,' I announced. 'Jock, use different dishes for lunch. Merry, get the bedrooms straightened. I'll be back as soon as I can.'

I left against a general wave of protest. What else could I do? No one was going to believe my suspicions concerning Susan unless I had some evidence. I exited the back door and made my way down the estate. There was a general air of dilapidation. The rough track was replete with weeds. I passed by one small cottage that was obviously uninhabited. Moss grew over the front step. The windows were no more than black eyes and the roof sagged alarmingly in the centre. As I moved farther away from the house I saw more and more deserted cottages. Some of them were, like the first, in a poor state, but a few were smarter and looked as if no more than a broom and a will were needed to put them straight. Yet all were empty.

Finally, at what now seemed a considerable distance from the house, I heard the sound of children laughing. I rounded a bend in the track and saw a scattering of cottages ahead. Smoke puffed from their chimneys and washing hung on the lines. I spotted a goat tethered on one side and, as I approached, a small, half-clad child ran screaming, but happy, past me.

As I drew nearer I saw these cottages too were in sore need of repair. There was also something of a smell. I knew only that Susan lived on the estate, so when the next merry urchin scurried past I called a question after it and flashed a bright penny. The penny was grabbed eagerly by one very dirty hand, while the other pointed at the second cottage on the right.

I had barely reached the front door before Susan came hurrying out. She attempted to pull the door shut behind her, but the wood had warped in the rain and I could clearly see that the cottage was fuller than its builders had intended. Before the door closed with a scrape and a bang, I glimpsed an older woman, dressed in black, scoop up the two merry urchins and push them farther inside.

'What is yous doing here?'

'You were meant to turn up for work this morning. We are very short-handed.'

'I thought after what had happened you wouldn't be wanting me back.'

I frowned. Was this a confession? 'So far I believe the incident is being treated as a terrible tragedy.'

'Terrible tragedy? Me stealing a bit of meat and bread for me bairns?'

'I am speaking of Mr Smith.'

The girl regarded me with her mouth shut firm in a stubborn line.

'You do know what happened at the shoot?'

'I don't know nothing about it,' Susan said crossing her arms in barricade before her. 'Mother and I and the bairns keeps ourselves to ourselves. Old Tom and his wife let us have the upstairs. It's too hard for them to get up there any more. No one's said they shouldn't. It's their let.' Her eyes sparkled with challenge.

'Oh, *children*,' I said, ignoring her aggressiveness. 'Do you also call them wains? I'm afraid I'm not at all familiar with Scottish words. Is that who you were speaking of the other day?'

She didn't respond.

'I have a little brother – Joe. He's many years my junior and always up to the most outrageous pranks. How old are yours?'

Susan's face softened slightly. 'Jimmy and Mhari, they're twins like, four.'

I smiled. 'I believe I've met them. The countryside is a great place for children to play.'

Susan's face hardened. 'Aye, maybe for them that has enough to eat. What do you want, Miss St John? What's happened now? What am I meant to have done this time?'

'Mr Smith has been killed at the shoot. The full circumstances are unclear.'

Susan sat down suddenly on the doorstep. 'Killed? I'm sorry. Did he have a family?'

'I don't know.'

'I hope not.' Susan stood up again. 'So you'll be needing me back?'

'I never asked you to leave.'

'But Jock said...'

'Jock should have said that incident could not be repeated. Lord Richard is a very different master to your last, by all accounts.'

'Aye, you can say that.'

'So you'll come back with me.'

'I'll tell Mother,' she said and pushed open the door. 'I am grateful,' she threw over her shoulder and disappeared swiftly inside.

Not many moments later she reappeared, a shawl wrapped around her shoulders. We began the long walk back in silence. As we approached the empty cottages I asked, 'What happened here?'

Susan shrugged. 'All I know is your Lord Richard had the pensioners removed from their homes.'

'Pensioners?'

'Widows, old folks, all those who'd had, or who'd been, folk working the estate. He let the main workers keep their cottages, but all the others were cleared out. Old Tom only kept his because Donal, who's taken over as gamekeeper, made out how he was vital to his job. Said he was an expert on culling.'

'I can see how that might appeal,' I muttered under my breath.

We walked on in silence. The sky began to drizzle. Susan pushed her shawl up over her head. The dark clouds above the house did nothing to dampen my imagination. As I stepped through the back door I sensed the tension and expectation in the air. I asked Susan to go to the scullery immediately and begin washing the dishes. I had told her

101

nothing of Rory's incarceration, not merely because I did not wish to dwell on the matter, but because my hopes were high, now that the mysterious Mr Edward had arrived, that Rory would already be released.

I found Jock clattering pans in the kitchen. 'I've brought Susan back with me,' I said.

'Aye.'

'Do you know if anything has transpired while I was away?'

'Has anything *transpired?*' asked Jock turning to face me and putting his hands on his hips. 'Has anything *transpired,* the wee lassie asks me! If you count Rory McLeod being formally charged with murder and tae be moved tomorrow to London, I would say a wee bit has transpired, aye. He wanted you to speak for him. It's too late now.'

'There's nothing I could have said,' I protested. 'You must be mistaken. The case against him is flimsy in the extreme.'

'I don't know about that. All I know is I've been told to ensure I have everything in order for a shooting luncheon tomorrow for the gentlemen are going back out once the butler is sent away.'

'This can't be happening,' I cried. I ran from the room with no thought in my head but to find Mr Bertram.

As my luck would have it he was alone in the library. 'You cannot let this happen,' I said rushing into the room and startling him into dropping ash on his newspaper. 'Rory is no killer.'

'Euphemia! Really! You cannot behave like this.'

'A man's life is at stake!'

'Oh, for heaven's sake, come in and shut the door before anyone else hears you.'

I did so and stood nervously twisting my hands together.

'Sit down,' said Mr Bertram. 'Would you like a small sherry?'

I managed to nod my head. It was such an extraordinary gesture on his behalf that I could not speak. He poured me what was indeed an extremely small sherry and held it out to me.

'Thank you.' I sipped daintily at the liquid. The fire that spread across my tongue was most welcome for I was still a trifle damp from the outside. However, as the liquor hit my stomach it reminded me in all the commotion that I had eaten no breakfast of my own. Mr Bertram pulled his chair opposite mine and sat down.

'Euphemia, I know you have imagined a fondness for Rory McLeod...'

I choked slightly. 'I hardly know him.'

'It is quite in character for one such as him to be adept at wheedling his way into the affections of the weaker sex.'

I set my glass down on a small table. 'Such a one? *Weaker sex?* When have I ever seemed weak to you?'

This brought a smile to his lips. 'I am well aware you are an extraordinary servant, Euphemia. I believe, once we have passed through this period of unpleasantness, you will find the situation of housekeeper far more suited to your talents than the lowly station of maid.'

'But he's innocent!'

'How can you possibly know?'

103

'There's no evidence.'

Mr Bertram began to tick the points off on his fingers. 'For no good reason, he left his position as loader to Mr Smith...'

'That was my fault.'

'I am sure that is what he wanted you to think. He even tried to call you to his defence. Is there anything you could have said that proved his innocence?' Mr Bertram regarded me with what I felt sure he thought was a kindly smile. I thought he looked infernally smug and my fingers itched to slap him.

'No,' I admitted, 'but you have said nothing to prove his guilt.'

Mr Bertram abandoned his point checking and sat back in his chair. He gave a deep sigh. 'It's more complicated than you imagine, Euphemia. I've known Smithy since I was his fag at school.' He must have seen my bemusement. 'It's an old-fashioned system, where a new boy must run and fetch for an older.'

My mind boggled at the thought of Mr Bertram fetching and carrying. 'Be his servant?'

'If you like, though it's not put in those terms. Anyway, it's not a nice thing to do. It's a rite of passage experience. The kind of thing that's meant to teach you your place.'

'Did Lord Richard do it too?' I asked fascinated.

'I presume so,' said Mr Bertram shortly. 'It's not to the point.'

I forgot myself so far as to snort.

'But Smithy,' continued Mr Bertram, 'was different. An absolute English gentleman. He couldn't have been kinder to me if we had been brothers.' He stopped. 'Actually he was a damn sight kinder. But the point is, he was a very decent fellow, perhaps the more so because he wasn't through-and-through English. His mother came from good stock, but his father was Korean. Something big in Korea back then, but he'd always carry the mark of not being quite British. It seemed to make him determined to be better at being British than the rest of us – and he was.'

'I'm sorry you lost your friend,' I said.

'So am I.'

We were both silent for a moment.

'Smith?'

Mr Bertram smiled. 'That was his father changing his name to fit in. Just like the ridiculous names they gave him.'

'His mother didn't have a say in it?'

'Apparently she adored his father. She must have, to marry him in the first place.'

'Poor woman. Are there other children?'

'A younger brother and sister.'

'It's all very sad, but even more unlikely a Scottish grocer's son would have a death wish against a half-Korean British gentleman. Surely their paths would never have crossed until today?'

'Probably not,' said Mr Bertram. 'But he's a communist, Euphemia, and the Japan-Korea Treaty of 1907 has never looked more shaky. It's a communist plot.'

'Communist assassins!' I said. 'You really believe that, after what happened with your own father? It's a line, Bertram, a line. It's what they say when they want people to look the other way.

Only this time there's a scapegoat – Rory.'

'No, Euphemia, you're wrong. I know last time it was just something that was said to close down the case, but the communist threat is real. The world is preparing for a war, the like of which no one has ever imagined. You don't understand the politics of the situation.'

'I might not understand politics, but I know Rory McLeod is no assassin,' I said.

'You're letting your heart rule your reason.'

'I am not!'

At this point we had both risen to our feet, pulsating with anger. Our bodies were in close enough proximity that I could feel the heat radiating from Mr Bertram. Our faces were inches from each other. Our eyes locked. My heart, generally a most reliable organ, turned over in my breast. Mr Bertram leaned slightly towards me. His voice was barely more than a whisper as he said, 'Euphemia...'

'Bertram...'

The door behind us opened and we sprang guiltily apart. 'What ho!' said Baggy Tipton with a leer.

I took the only course open to me and fled from the room. As my readers will understand, my thoughts were in turmoil for the rest of the day and barely worth recording. Suffice it to say, my fallible mind played over and over the final scene with Mr Bertram although it dared go no further than the actualities that occurred. My reaction to the situation was unnerving. I was more than aware that I had called Mr Bertram by his Christian name now on several occasions. Of course, had I been present in his house as myself, Euphemia Martins, not only a vicar's daughter but also the granddaughter of an earl – if my grandfather ever took it upon himself to acknowledge me or my brother – he might have considered himself fortunate to be on such terms with me. If my grandfather ever accepted my mother back into the family then I would be openly his social superior. As matters stood within my family our social standing was, to put it mildly, confused. While I worked under a false identity as a maid – or housekeeper – I had no excuse whatsoever to address a gentleman of the house by his first name. I could only suppose that I had done so because, of all of them, Bertram had recognised something in me. He did not treat me as an equal and yet he did not treat me as a servant. At least I, knowing what I really was, understood the confusion this had engendered between us. Bertram, on the other hand, had no such advantage and I could only come to one conclusion over his extraordinary behaviour. He was jealous of Rory.

I will not flatter myself that he was in love with me, but I was enough out of the norm, yet as Little Joe says: 'pretty, even for a sister', and we were in the vast isolation of Scotland, and there lay between us the history of our previous adventures investigating murders – it was no wonder that passions were being stirred.

How in all this mess could I help Rory? I was convinced he was not a killer and the one man I would have turned to as an ally was blinded by unreasonable prejudice. That Euphemia Martins would have feelings for a grocer's son was unthinkable – and yet my innate honesty, instilled in me by my lovely and wise father, forced me to consider that my extremely aristocratic mother married far beneath her station. Could this be a family trait?

But when I thought of my parting with Bertram, *Mr Bertram*, as I must call him even to myself, my chest hurt.

I went about my duties in a daze and, because I was not worrying over their correct performance, did them so excellently that I even earned praise from Lord Richard. I avoided seeing Mr Bertram.

I retired to bed once more in a state of extreme exhaustion and with my mind raging with energy. It took me some considerable time to achieve a state of slumber and I could not long have entered it when I was awoken by a loud crash.

I awoke instantly, all my nerves tingling. A few moments later there was a blinding flash of light and then, shortly after, another crash. Rain was pelting the windows with an almost preternatural ferocity and it was clear a thunderstorm of epic proportions was centred near the lodge.

I am not generally afraid of nature, but this was a most fearful storm. To my bemusement Merry slept on, so I pulled the covers up to my chin and determined to wait the storm out. It was likely only a quarter of an hour, although it felt like very much more, when the time between lightning and thunder began to lengthen. I was inwardly sighing with relief and attempting to compose my mind to enter sleep when I became aware of a lesser noise somewhere deep within the house.

It was not the insistent banging of an open door like the other night, but rather the sounds that might be made by someone creeping through the house. Two thoughts leapt to the forefront of my mind. It was either Susan returning to pilfer the pantry once more or it was Rory attempting to escape. It seemed the height of foolishness to consider a burglar would put himself to the inconvenience of travelling out to a remote lodge such as this one, particularly on a night so fearful.

It was clear then that I was the one to deal with whatever lay below. I slipped out of bed and wrapped my housecoat tightly around me. I put my housekeeping keys in my pocket in case I needed to relock any of the doors and set forth. I was not sure what I would do if I came upon Rory in midescape, but it would not be the first time I had aided a criminal in flight. However, last time I was in no doubt it was the morally correct action to take. This time, I did not know.

I crept quickly down the stairs, sheltering my candle flame, and ignoring the flickering shadows as best I could. If it were Susan, it was essential I found her before either of the Stapleford brothers. Though what I would do with her, again I did not know. I had already warned her once.

It did not escape my sense of irony that, whatever I found below, I would have to make a morally difficult choice and that I was currently more concerned over thievery than murder.

What I did not consider, until I reached the kitchens, was that it might be someone other than Rory and any accomplice abroad. It might be the real murderer!

I came around the passage towards the pantries with my shadow towering before me. It was then I heard a scraping noise. Someone was indeed trying to break into the food supplies. I let out a cry of 'Hi!' and ran forward. The candle flame flickered and died, but not before I saw quite clearly the main pantry remained shuttered and locked.

There was the sound of feet running away from me. I put my hands against the walls and moved forward as quickly as I dared in the dark. I realised now someone had been trying to break into the pantry that served as Rory's cell. I rounded the corner and a flash of light illuminated the pantry door. There were scratches all around the lock. Trembling, I took the keys from my pocket and unlocked the door and opened it.

Another flash of light illuminated Rory, a small stool above his head about to rush forth and strike. I cried out and raised my hands above my head. A moment later I felt his warm arms around me.

'Euphemia, thank God,' breathed his voice in my ear. 'Someone was trying to break in here. I think they wanted to kill me.'

I broke free from his embrace and shut the door behind us and locked it. The lightning flashed once more and I saw a slow smile creep across his face.

'They might still be outside,' I said.

'You believe I'm innocent?'

'Of course.'

'Ah, Euphemia, but you're a grand lass,' said

Rory catching me up in his embrace once more. To his credit, he did not try to kiss me and I determined he was simply overly relieved that someone believed in him. I broke free once more, but this time more gently. I noted for reference, purely to prevent any possible future escape, that his arms were pleasingly muscular for a man I had seen lift nothing heavier than a tray.

'We need to talk,' I said. 'There has been a serious allegation laid against you that you are a member of the communist party.'

'I think the one of murder is a mite more serious,' said Rory.

'They're saying you killed because you're a communist. Are you?'

'No – that is ... I suppose I am still technically a member of the party...'

'Oh, Rory!'

'But I only joined because Jenny Roberts was a member and I fancied myself in love with her.'

'Are you still in love with her?' I demanded, involuntarily stamping my foot.

'No, of course not,' said Rory. 'What's more to the point, I've no interest in politics whatsoever.'

'When did you last go to a meeting?'

'Years ago,' said Rory. 'It was back in my days as a callow youth.'

'As opposed to your present declining years,' I said smiling.

'I'm afraid, Euphemia, that my decline might be extremely rapid, if not short, on the end of a rope.'

'I will not allow that to happen,' I said.

'I'd be happy to think you can help,' said Rory,

'but I'm not sure there is much you can do.'

'Did you explain to Mr Edward about your association with the communists and the reason for it?'

'Who is Mr Edward?'

'The investigator. He hasn't even been to see you? That is very strange.'

'I reckon he thinks it's a done deal.'

'Then I will enlighten him,' I said.

'I'd appreciate any help, but don't put yourself in danger, Euphemia. Remember there is a real murderer out there.'

'You might even say you are in the safest spot.' I laughed.

'You're welcome to share it with me.'

'I think not,' I said gently. 'It would be very difficult once things returned to normal in the household. Besides, I was brought up quite strictly.'

'All the girls worth knowing are,' said Rory, I thought a trifle sadly.

'We are overly emotional and it is no wonder,' said as much to myself as to Rory. 'I will speak to people in the morning and make them understand they have made a mistake.'

The lightning had not flashed for some time, but it did now and I saw the slow, sad smile spread over Rory's handsome face. 'You're a grand lass, Euphemia, but don't put your head in a noose for me. If you start pointing out the error of their ways they might decide we were in it together.'

I drew myself up to my full height in a good impersonation of my mother, 'Just let them try,' I said in dire accents.

Rory laughed and before I could stop him

darted forward and planted a swift kiss on my cheek. 'That's for luck,' he said.

I did not trust myself to speak, so I let myself out without a word and locked him in once more. I decided against lighting the candle from the stove and instead made my way quickly up the main staircase. Dawn was near and there was sufficient light if I was careful.

More than once, my hand stole to my cheek. It was as if his lips had imprinted themselves upon my flesh. There was undoubtedly a connection between us.

I paused on the landing and looked out at the beginning of the new day. What I saw brought a smile to my lips. For once, the elements had worked in our favour. There was no possibility of a trap or automobile leaving the house tomorrow. The storm had washed the drive clear away. Rory was safe for now. I had one more day to prove his innocence and I determined that was exactly what I would do.

Chapter Six

The Enigmatic Mr Fitzroy

Preparations for breakfast had hardly begun before Mr Bertram strode into the kitchen and demanded men.

'I want every able-bodied man on the staff, Euphemia, dressed suitably and out in front of the house in 20 minutes. We need to shore up the drive.'

'Is there not time for breakfast, sir?' I asked. 'It looked to me as if most of the drive had already gone and the weather is very bad still.'

Mr Bertram glowered at me. 'That's the point, Euphemia. We've lost the top section of the drive already. If the underpinning layers go too it will take weeks to repair and we'll all be stuck here.' He frowned even more heavily. 'As if that wouldn't suit you!'

'Indeed, sir,' I said. 'I can assure you I have no desire to stay at the lodge for longer than the dates already agreed. In fact, I would dare to assume that the majority of the inhabitants of this house, who are at liberty to leave, would wish to do so as soon as possible.'

'Exactly,' said Mr Bertram.

I flushed as I finally understood his meaning. 'About that, sir, if I could have a word in private. I do feel that a mistake has...'

Mr Bertram raised his hand, cutting me off. 'Enough, Miss St John. I know where your sympathies lie, but there is nothing I can do to help.'

'But, sir...' I started.

Mr Bertram turned on me with a snarl that would have done credit to his brother, 'I said enough!' he barked.

I started backwards at the loudness of his reprimand and, to my horror, felt tears sting my eyes.

'Get the men out there now.'

'Would they no work the harder with a bit of breakfast inside them?' asked Jock, who had been listening quietly.

'There is no time,' said Mr Bertram.

'If you don't mind me saying,' said Mr Fitzroy, 'I think that is a mistake. A man with a good breakfast inside him will achieve more in two hours than a hungry man will in five.'

We all jumped at the sound of his voice. He was standing at the entrance to the kitchen, a rain cape over his arm. 'Sorry if I startled you,' he said with a smile. 'I took the liberty of seeing if the storage rooms could provide any heavy weather gear. I presumed none of the other guests would have brought such. One doesn't generally shoot in this kind of weather.'

'Indeed,' said Mr Bertram, turning his back to me, and speaking in quite a different voice he said, 'I wouldn't be surprised if my brother tries to get some of his purchase price back from the seller! I don't think he counted on the weather being quite so inclement.'

'It's rare for it to be as bad as this, sirs!' objected Jock.

'I was joking,' said Mr Bertram. 'But I take Mr Fitzroy's point. The men will be better workers with breakfast inside them. I will bow to his judgement. Ensure everyone is well-fed, but not too well-fed, Euphemia.'

He didn't even look at me as he gave the order. I boiled with fury. The suggestion was acceptable from Fitzroy, but not from me! Mr Bertram left the kitchen leaving me facing Mr Fitzroy. Jock turned back to his pots and began clattering them alarmingly.

'Perhaps, I might have a word, Miss St John? Somewhere more quiet?'

I led him through to the housekeeper's parlour. I wasn't entirely sure if this was suitable but, really, I am becoming rather resigned to having a reputation that is unfairly tarnished. Mr Fitzroy sat down in a comfy chair close to my tiny fire and said without preamble, 'Why, exactly, do you not believe Rory McLeod is our murderer?'

'The evidence against him is circumstantial,' I said.

'But strong,' said Mr Fitzroy.

'He only joined the communist party to impress a young woman.'

'Well, men have done stranger things to impress members of the opposite sex,' he said with a smile. 'But we only have his word for this, I take it? And who is to say that once he joined he might not have become attracted by their ideals?'

'But he's not like that!'

Mr Fitzroy crossed his legs and settled back in his seat. 'And what is he like?'

'What's he like?' I repeated blankly. 'I've only known him a few days.'

'But already he appears to have made a strong impression on you. So I repeat my question: what is he like?'

'He's keen to run an orderly house,' I said, thinking. 'He expects his staff to be above reproach, but he's fair. If he makes a mistake, he owns it rather than blaming another. He's very observant and intelligent. He takes his position very seriously. At all times, he acts with honour and integrity.'

'A glowing reference,' said Mr Fitzroy. 'He is, though I am no real judge of these things, also a handsome man. Could you, if I required, provide anecdotal evidence of the credits you list?'

'When we first met,' I began.

'I only need a yes or no,' interrupted Mr Fitzroy. 'Please think carefully, Euphemia. I suspect that you are not entirely unaffected by McLeod's charm. Remember justice is blind for a reason.'

I sighed. 'You believe me to be biased.'

'I do, but I also believe you are capable of standing back from that bias and answering my question truthfully. Have you seen signs of the virtues you ascribe to McLeod or are they more fantasy than fact?'

I took a moment to consider the question. 'In all honesty, Mr Fitzroy, it is difficult to be precise. I have observed actions that correspond to all the attributes I have listed, but it is more than that. My instincts tell me he is innocent. But what good does that do him?'

'What do your instincts tell you of the other men here?'

'Sir?'

'What do you think of Max Tipton?'

I cannot explain why, but I sensed my answer to his question would determine Rory's fate and so I was more frank than I might otherwise have been about those who I was pretending were my social superiors.

'He's a weak man with little courage and an overfondness for female company. I suspect he is quite libidinous! He does not seem popular with the others, but tolerated through long association. I heard him arguing with Lord Richard, accusing him of not returning either money or favours.'

117

'Did you indeed!' said Mr Fitzroy. 'What about Muller?'

'He frightens me a little,' I confessed. 'Though I can't say why. He is older than the others and yet chooses to associate with the younger men. I imagine it gives him an added feeling of importance. I believe he works in the city. I suspect he is not as successful as he would like.'

Mr Fitzroy laughed out loud and clapped. 'Bertram?'

'I believe him to be an honourable, intelligent man, who is occasionally overruled by his passions and ideals.'

Fitzroy raised an eyebrow. 'You know him well?'

I felt myself blush. 'Not that well,' I said meaningfully.

He nodded. 'I know that,' he said. 'Richard?'

'He is my employer.'

'Come now, Euphemia, this is not the occasion for shyness.'

'Very well.' I took a deep breath. 'I believe him to be an ambitious man of dubious morals, who cares for his own advancement above all else. He is of a choleric nature and, while not overly intelligent, he has a cunningness that many underestimate.'

'McGillvary?'

'I know little of him. Upon his arrival, he smoothed over a row between the staff. He appears more socially skilled than the others. He insulted Lord Richard, but so subtly it had to be taken as a joke. I think he is one of the cleverest, but I have no real impression of his character.'

'The late Mr Smith?'

'He seemed a very nice and kind gentleman,' I said sadly.

'And last, but not least, myself?'

'You confuse me, sir. You have changed many times in apparent personality since you arrived. One minute you are extremely approachable, the next quite intimidating. I do not think you are exactly what you claim to be, but what you are I do not know.'

'I must be slipping,' muttered Fitzroy. Then to me he said, 'Your observations are, for the main part, acute. However, there is nothing in what you say to help McLeod and we both agree the evidence against him, though circumstantial, is strong.'

'What can we do?' I asked.

'I don't believe Edward believes this to be the open-and-shut case the others would like. There remain other avenues, at least some of which may be easier for you than the others to explore.'

'Will you help me, sir?'

Fitzroy rose to his feet. 'No, but if you do decide to pursue matters yourself, I would advise you to have any incidents witnessed and to be careful not to expose yourself to danger.'

'But, sir, won't you help me? What was the point of all these questions if...'

I trailed off under his cold gaze. I saw intelligence and calculation in his grey eyes, but the warmth of earlier had quite vanished. 'I wish you a good morning, Euphemia,' he said and departed.

The door closed and I was left in silence. I became aware of the rain once more lashing against the window and the crackle of the little fire, but most of all the thumping of my heart. I realised that during my conversation with Mr Fitzroy I had actually been rather afraid. I could not explain this, as his manner for the majority of the time had been most friendly, but with his departure I found myself flooded with relief rather like a lion-tamer, who once more walks out of the cage alive at the end of a performance.

There was a tap on my door and Merry poked her head round. 'Euphemia...'

'Merry, come in. I need to ask you something.' Merry's eyes widened in her freckled face, but she entered and closed the door softly behind her.

'I need your help,' I said bluntly. 'I don't believe Rory McLeod is guilty and I intend to prove it.'

Whatever reaction I might have anticipated to my announcement tears did not come uppermost in my expectations. I was astonished when Merry collapsed weeping to the ground. 'I'm so sorry,' she gasped between sobs. 'It's all my fault.'

I went over and helped her to a chair. 'Don't be ridiculous. It can't possibly be your fault, Merry. Unless you're trying to tell me you killed Mr Smith yourself.'

'I did as good as. It was me what gave him the wrong cartridges. That's why his gun blew up, isn't it? That's what Willie said. He had the wrong stuff and it's my fault.' Merry began to wail.

I had prior experience of Merry's wailing. If I were being unkind, I might say it is one of her most notable skills. It is certainly not something to which anyone would ever wish to be subjected.

I slapped her smartly around the face. This brought the noise to an abrupt end.

'You had better explain exactly what you mean,' I said. 'This is a most serious situation.'

'They'll hang me for sure,' said Merry. She inhaled deeply as if in preparation for another noisy exhalation.

'The next time I slap you it will be much harder.'

Merry stopped short.

'Explain yourself.'

Merry gulped. 'Do you remember the morning of the shoot I was up a long time before you?' she said in a tiny voice.

I nodded.

'I was meeting someone. I'd got speaking to one of the local lads and 'e reckoned how the morning light's real special up here. He offered to show me.'

'Oh, Merry!'

'Oh, no! It ain't nothing like that. He really did take me and show me a view.'

My ears were quick to detect a note of regret. 'And he asked you to add something to Mr Smith's bag?'

'Jamie! No, never! He's got nothing to do with this.'

'Then why mention him?' I asked exasperated.

''Cos I was tired, like, from getting up so early. I knew I'd let you down the other day – so, even though I felt like sneaking off for a kip, I reckoned the least I could do was get an early start of them bags and stuff that were going up for the shoot. I were sorting 'em all out into the right piles when Susan turned up. She said I'd got everything in a

121

right guddle – whatever that is – and she tried to help me put 'em straight, but I must have got 'em too wrong. I must have given Mr Smith the wrong bag and that's how he got the wrong cartridges for 'is gun.' Merry inhaled.

I put up my hand. 'You were sorting cartridges?'

'Nah, we were putting all the gentlemen's stuff together like the notes Mr McLeod had left out. Flask of tea for Mr Smith. Flask of whisky for Lord Richard. Hand-warmers for Mr McGillvary. Putting all their stuff together, shooting sticks, all that kind of thing. Mr McLeod's idea was that each of their stuff be loaded into a separate wicker basket so it was easy to sort out the other end and get on with the shooting straight off.' She raised her tearstained face to me. 'I killed him. Sure as if I'd shot him myself.'

'No, wait a minute, Merry. You sorted the bags into the different baskets.'

'Yeah, I must have mixed 'em up.'

'But you didn't touch any of the cartridges?'

'No.'

'I heard Mr Edward ask Mr Bertram about that. He said the cartridges Mr Smith got shouldn't have been on the premises at all. Mr Bertram said they must have been the ones meant for his sister, if she'd come.'

'But there weren't no basket for her. She's not here.'

'Don't you see, Merry? All the men were using the same cartridge size. Mr Smith's gun was no different in size to the others.'

'You mean someone deliberately put them in

122

poor Mr Smith's bag to kill him?' asked Merry shocked.

'But you're not sure you gave Mr Smith the right bag, are you?'

'Oh, gawd! You mean, I might have helped kill the wrong man!'

'Merry, you didn't kill anyone. Whoever put those cartridges in a bag certainly intended to kill someone. It's not your fault. You didn't mean any harm. You didn't know.'

'But they might have meant to kill someone different.'

'Perhaps,' I said cautiously.

'Well, I sure as 'ell wish they'd ended up in Lord Richard's bag rather than that nice Mr Smith.'

'Merry! That's a terrible thing to say.'

'All I'm saying is, if one of them had to die, I'd rather it had been 'im.'

I sat down. 'I need to think. This could change everything. If the murderer didn't kill the person he meant to,' I stopped. 'Did you say Susan was helping you?'

'Yeah. She can be a bit stuck up, but she was right helpful that morning.'

'Hmm,' I said. 'As helpful as when she forgot to wipe the beeswax on the stairs when she thought Lord Richard was about to come down.'

'You don't mean she's the murderer,' whispered Merry in thrilled accents. 'How terrible.' Her eyes glowed with excitement.

'I don't know,' I said sternly. 'I don't want you repeating any of this until we can find out the truth.'

'Mum's the word,' said Merry her eyes as big as

dinner plates. 'What are you going to do?'

'Susan said how Lord Richard had turned people out of their cottages, but she didn't explain what happened to her.'

'I reckon Jamie would know,' said Merry eagerly.

I smiled. 'That's what I thought. Can you ask him discreetly?'

''Course I can. He's a nice lad, even if he is a one for views.'

'Merry, I thought you had family in the country. I thought you grew up in the country?'

'Nah, I was one too many for me Ma. I was sent off to an aunt in the city. Stapleford Hall's the only country I've ever known – and it doesn't exactly give you a taste for it, if you see what I mean.'

I did, but it was more urgent that I got on with the business of the day. So I made Merry dry her face, compelled her to secrecy and sent her on her way. I had been away far longer than I intended. When I arrived back at the kitchen there were a hundred and one tasks to oversee. I could almost understand why Mrs Wilson, on occasion, took to the bottle. If I never see another cheeky delivery boy, it will be too soon. The isolation of the lodge gave us little choice in the matter of milk, egg and even bread suppliers – Jock, perversely refused to make bread. What with this and the current absence of a front drive, which he would not have been allowed to use anyway, seemed to make the local boy think he was entitled to a handsome gratuity, simply for doing his job.

However annoying this and the overseeing of the domestic chores were, the low point of my morning came when Willie brought me the news that I was required to serve at luncheon. I pointed out that this was not in the normal role of a housekeeper and Willie reminded me that, in the informality of the lodge, Rory had waited on some meals.

'Can't you manage on your own?' I asked him.

'If you excuse my saying so, miss, they is difficult gentlemen.'

I sighed, tacitly acknowledging the truth of this. 'Well, get another of the Stapleford men to help you.'

'There isn't another who's trained at table service, miss.'

'Well, these are extraordinary circumstances. I'm sure the gentlemen will understand.'

'They're all too scared,' confessed Willie.

It took me a moment to understand he was referring to the staff and not the guests.

'I'm not too keen myself,' said Willie. 'If there were anyone else. But I don't want to let you down, miss.' Normally the sight of a six-foot-tall footman swallowing manfully would have made me giggle, but I sensed Willie was truly full of trepidation.

It occurred to me at this moment that, with Rory's incarceration, domestic details were the least of my worries. I really should have foreseen the crisis of morale that was obviously rampant. 'How foolish,' I said. 'Of course I will serve.' My father would have been proud at my decision to lead from the front.

It had also occurred to me that I might overhear something of interest.

I realised how greatly I had been mistaken when I entered with the soup tureen. Both my hands were occupied with holding the dish and Willie was serving. When we left the kitchen it had seemed the better plan as I had no experience of pouring soup onto the plates from standing and I was uncertain of hitting my target. However, I quickly saw how Tipton's gaze was following me in a most ungentlemanly manner. His surveyed me from my head to my heels in such a way as I found myself blushing furiously. I also had no hands to defend myself. I angled my body as far away from him as possible as Willie served him, so I was quite unprepared when I received a hearty smack on my posterior from Mr Muller.

I think it is not unsurprising that I squealed and dropped the tureen. The gentlemen broke into laughter. All except Mr Bertram, who remonstrated with Mr Muller in the most ungentlemanly language, but so strongly on my behalf that I could not but be grateful.

'Oh come on, Bertie,' said Lord Richard. 'No maid ever objected to a bit of slap and tickle.'

'She's not a maid. Euphemia is your housekeeper,' said Bertram in strangled accents as he attempted to rein in his temper.

'Still not entirely sure she's only working for me,' said Lord Richard nodding at Bertram and winking at the others.

'Dickie, that is unconscionable and uncalled for,' said Bertram.

'Who'd have thought it would be little Bertie who'd turn out to be the ladies' man,' said

McGillvary. 'When we were all at school he was the shyest of the lot of us.'

'I am not,' began Bertram hotly.

'But fie on you, Muller! You were our head boy! You should be setting a dashed sight better example to us younger ones,' shouted McGillvary, laughing at some old joke.

'Thought I *was* setting the right damned example,' said Muller. I noticed now his face was flushed with wine.

Lord Richard shouted with laughter.

'But I didn't get any soup,' complained Tipton. 'It's all over the floor.'

There was more laughter.

'Perhaps, gentlemen, in the spirit of eating rather than spilling luncheon, we might leave assailing the staff until later,' said Mr Fitzroy. 'I have brought an appetite to the table.'

'*So have I!*' cried Muller and they all laughed again.

I took this as my cue to exit. As far as I was concerned they would have to deal with the necessarily slower service Willie alone could offer them.

After lunch the men decided to go out. I have no idea where they were going and at this point I had no interest in seeing any of them save Mr Bertram again. However, Mother and Little Joe were counting on me so, once I was assured by Willie that they really had left, I went upstairs to see what could be done about the soup stain on the carpet. I was kneeling on the floor in a most vulnerable position when I heard the door behind me open.

'You do put yourself in these awkward situ-

127

ations, don't you?' said Mr Fitzroy.

I sprang up and turned angrily upon him. I had not forgotten that he had laughed at my distress earlier. 'I don't know what you mean by that, sir,' I said through gritted teeth.

'For an intelligent girl, you certainly do and say the most foolish things,' said Fitzroy helping himself to a cigar from the sideboard. 'If I had been one of the others...'

'I made sure the guests had gone out before I came upstairs,' I said.

'But I hadn't.'

'These precautions should not be necessary in a gentleman's house!' I cried.

Mr Fitzroy took an implement from his pocket and punctured his cigar. 'There is a difference,' he said mildly, 'between those born into the ranks and those whose parents got them there with finance. I don't believe you will find an honourable saying over the Stapleford hearth.'

'All those men went to school together,' I said, 'and now they are powerful and rich – and doesn't that strike you as a strange coincidence?'

Fitzroy threw back his head and laughed. 'Oh, Euphemia, in some ways you are so sharp and in others so extremely naive. That, my dear, is how the world works.'

'Well, it shouldn't,' I said.

'I will tell you this. In my experience, the key to a situation lies with the true character and background of all those involved. What do you know of Mr Smith?'

'Very little.'

'Is there no one you could ask?'

'No one who would talk to me,' I said bitterly.

'Ah, that is a shame.'

'Locking Rory up as a communist is ridiculous! It makes no sense.'

'It seems to me there are all too many communists abroad in this country when you are involved.'

I blanched. 'Are you accusing me of being a Bolshevik?'

'I wouldn't be the first, would I, Miss St John? Or should I say Miss Martins? Daughter of the late Rev Joshia Martins of Sweetfield Parish and granddaughter of–'

At this juncture I fled from the room fearing all was discovered.

Chapter Seven

Local Suspicion

I was packing in our bedchamber when Merry burst into the room. 'I 'ave news,' she said dramatically.

'You will have to tell it to Mr Bertram,' I said shutting my case. 'I don't work here any more.'

'What?' screeched Merry. 'You can't! You can't leave me 'ere alone with this lot!'

I began checking through the chest of drawers to ensure I hadn't left any of my meagre possessions behind. 'I have to,' I said in a thick voice.

'What's he done? Who's done it? I'll kill 'im!'

'I can't explain,' I said finding the bottom of an empty drawer suddenly very interesting. I felt Merry's arm go round my shoulders. 'You can tell me,' she said. 'I know how we've had our differences from time to time, but we're the same, you and I. Us against this lot.'

I was much moved by Merry's speech, but there was no way I could in honesty answer it. 'What did you find out?' I asked, hoping to divert her.

'Well,' said Merry breathlessly, 'you know how Lord Richard heaved a lot of the estate tenants out of their cottages? Turns out one of them was Susan's father.'

'That's very sad, but it doesn't give her a motive more than any of the others he dispossessed.'

'But he died!'

'What?'

'He 'ad an 'eart attack and died. Susan blames Lord Richard for it.'

'That's terrible.'

'He's a mean old sod at the best of times, but turfing old folks out? I wouldn't have blamed 'er if she'd murdered 'im. Just a pity she got Mr Smith by mistake.'

'Merry, we don't know that.'

'There's more.'

I waited. 'What is it?'

Merry shrugged. 'I don't know. Jamie got called away. I can try and catch him later. Only if you want, that is.' Merry tried to look demure and failed.

'You'll have to tell this all to Mr Bertram,' I said.

130

'I can't,' said Merry. 'I can't talk to one of them. That's what you do.'

'But I'm leaving!'

'You're going to leave an innocent man to hang?'

'No, but you can tell them.'

'I'm not the one Mr Bertram listens to.'

'Try Mr Fitzroy or one of the others then.'

'Euphemia, they don't listen to maids. That lot never do. For some reason you can make them pay attention to you, but you're odd. No one will pay any attention to me.'

My heart sank. I knew she was right. 'I'll speak to someone before I go,' I said quietly.

'Just mind it's someone with sense,' said Merry. 'Maybe they'll be able to talk some into you.'

There seemed no reason to extend my time under this roof, so I gently suggested Merry should go about her tasks and made my way downstairs in the hope of finding Mr Bertram. However, the other gentlemen had not returned, and it was Mr Fitzroy I found at his ease reading a paper in front of the fire in the first floor library.

At my entrance he peeled down a corner of the paper and regarded me. 'Were you looking for me?'

'I have further information that may have a bearing on the murder case,' I said. 'I have evidence that points in quite another direction from Mr McLeod.'

'Then you should tell Mr Edward. I believe he will be here this evening. It's his department.'

'I shall be leaving shortly. Your knowledge of my identity makes it impossible for me to remain,' I said stiffly.

'Now, don't be petulant, Euphemia. I haven't told anyone,' said Mr Fitzroy. 'Nor do I have any intention of so doing.'

'Then why? How?'

Mr Fitzroy folded his paper. 'Would you say your secret detrimentally affects the Staplefords?'

I shook my head.

'I also have a secret, which I believe you have begun to suspect. My secret also does not detrimentally affect the Staplefords.'

'A stand-off,' I said, swallowing. 'You have it in your power to blackmail me.' I am sure the disgust I felt showed on my face.

Mr Fitzroy smiled. 'It really is quite a delight to come across someone with such quick wits. It is so rare among the upper classes. From your face I can tell you think I am no gentleman and you are quite correct. However, I play fair,' the smile broadened, 'for the most part. For what it is worth I would much rather you had been no more than a devilishly quick-witted maid. Your status and in particular your relations tie my hands in dealing with you.'

'I can assure you my grandfather takes no interest in me.'

'More fool him,' said Mr Fitzroy. 'Let us agree, then, to leave each other in peace. I shall go on with my work and you can go on with yours – both the housekeeping and the detecting. In fact, I am afraid I must insist on the latter. It's really not in my role to go barging in and if you do have further information you will need to supply it to the authorities.' He looked at me very levelly. 'Do

132

you understand?'

'I don't have a choice, do I?'

'Let us say of the alternatives before you it would seem the least unpleasant.'

'Then I will bid you good day, sir,' I said. I walked out with as much dignity as I could muster, but I was sure I heard the echo of laughter behind me. It was clear Mr Fitzroy had enjoyed the interview far more than I had. I was still thinking what I could do, when I heard the front door bang. I peered over the landing rail and saw it was the gentlemen returning. Most of them headed through to the downstairs rooms, but Mr Bertram, who was looking particularly muddy, broke off and headed up the stairs. I decided to waylay him on the landing.

'Mr Bertram, I must talk to you.'

'Good heavens, Euphemia. You'll give me a heart attack jumping out like that. If you'll excuse me, I must go and change.' He set off at a smart pace towards his room.

'I must speak to you.'

Mr Bertram ignored me and opened the door to his room. I followed him in. 'Really, Euphemia! This is not seemly! Leave at once.'

I placed my back against the door. 'I need to speak to you. It's about Rory.'

'I should have known! I can only advise you to disengage your affections and employ your reason!'

'But I have new evidence.'

'Evidence, or below-stairs tittle-tattle? Have you learnt nothing from our previous unfortunate mis-adventure? It is not our business to meddle in

133

these affairs.'

'Because the police do such a good job? We both know that not to be the case.'

'This is different,' snapped Mr Bertram. 'There are forces at work here of which you can have no notion. You must stay out of it. That is an order!'

'You think you can order me to disregard my sense of justice,' I cried hotly, my breast heaving with indignation.

'I think if you want to keep your job you will refrain from interfering.'

'That's to be my excuse, is it? What's yours?'

'What?' Mr Bertram pulled off his tie with a snap. 'If you have any care to your reputation, I suggest you leave. I intend to disrobe.'

'Lord Richard. We both know what he is. Did you know his latest exploits included throwing estate workers out of their homes? Or did you help him do it?'

Mr Bertram had the grace to blush. 'I have had no say in the management of this estate.'

'So you wouldn't know anything about a young woman whose father died of a heart attack shortly after he was turned out the cottage he'd lived in all his life? I'd say that was an excellent motive for murder.'

Mr Bertram swallowed. 'I assure you, I know nothing about this.'

'No,' I said scornfully, 'you merely dine at your brother's table, live in his house...'

'It is not his house,' said Mr Bertram hotly.

'Stapleford Hall belonged to your mother?' I asked, suddenly wondering if I had misjudged him.

'It was left for the use of her children. The first of us to have a legitimate heir, provided we remain living at the hall, will inherit it and a trust fund dedicated to its maintenance.'

I felt as if the breath had been knocked out of me.

'That is why I was able to convince Richard to keep you on. I have equal say in the running of the house.'

'Am I meant to thank you for that?' I gasped. 'You, who would live with that man, after what he has done, in the house built from blood money on the chance of inheriting it? You, who have your own income?'

'My income is none of your business. Besides it would never enable me to afford the upkeep of such a property.'

'I had thought better of you,' I said quietly.

'Euphemia, you have no right to judge me!'

'No, though I do have every right to ask for your help in seeing justice done, but I see now your actions and morals are tempered by your worldly desires. I had thought you different from most men in that respect.'

'This is completely and utterly inappropriate. I will not be spoken to in this manner by a servant.'

'I apologise, sir. I now realise I was completely in error to ask you to be of aid. I need to find a gentleman of honour.'

Mr Bertram, who had been quite red with anger, now turned alarmingly white. I did not wait to hear what he had to say.

I fairly ran out of the room. My blood was up and I undoubtedly looked somewhat wild-eyed. I knew myself to be on the verge of hysterical tears, but I also knew I could waste no more time. Accordingly, when I saw Mr Edward enter the library I followed him.

'Excuse me, sir. I have evidence that may lead you to reconsider your arrest of Mr McLeod,' I said in a rush before he had even sat down.

Mr Edward poured himself a whisky and sat down in the armchair previously occupied by Mr Fitzroy. He took his time. I barely restrained myself from hopping from foot to foot. 'Who are you, young lady?'

'Euphemia St John, sir, the housekeeper.'

There was a slight cough at this and I realised that Mr Fitzroy had not departed the room, but merely moved a little away from the fire, which by this time was roaring nicely.

Mr Edward reached out his hands to the fire. 'Scotland – all four seasons in one day,' he murmured to himself. 'Why the devil should I listen to a word you have to say, young woman? Does Lord Richard normally let you disturb his guests?'

'It is a matter of justice,' I said levelly.

'More likely a case of handsome butler and a pretty, foolish wench,' said Mr Edward.

'You should listen to her, Edward,' said Mr Fitzroy unexpectedly. 'She has a good mind.'

Mr Edward settled back in his chair and sipped his whisky. He crossed one leg over the other and surveyed me for a moment. He had a most unremarkable, even bland face, but for the first time I noticed his eyes were very dark – almost black. I fancied I could see the flames of the firelight flicker across their depths in a most

136

unnerving fashion. The shadowy gaze was unpleasant, but I also felt as if – and it is hard to find the right words – as if I was being looked into and fully observed. And yet, it was not the steadiness of his gaze that particularly disturbed me. It was that it was wholly dispassionate, cold and calculating. It took all of my will not to fidget under his examination, but I stood firm and thought of my mother staring down the butcher to whom she owed so much money.

Mr Edward shrugged. 'Well, if Fitzroy thinks I should listen to you. Speak, girl. Make it quick.'

I thought for a moment and then presented my thoughts quickly and as neatly as I could.

'One of the local women who works on the estate has a serious grudge against Lord Richard. He has forcibly evicted a number of tenants from their cottages, including her own father, who died shortly afterwards of a heart attack. On our first day here, she apparently forgot to wipe the wax polish off the main stairs and a serious accident was only prevented by chance. On the morning of the shoot she was eager to help one of our maids, Merry, sort out the gentlemen's kit for the shoot. This was entirely out of character, as previously she had been surly and reluctant to be of service.

'I suspect her to be a woman deeply disturbed by grief and a desire for revenge. I believe in both cases she intended Lord Richard to be her target, but her planning and execution is beyond her natural abilities, and that Mr Smith erroneously became her victim. Moreover, I have been assured by Mr McLeod that his membership of the communist party was a foolish lovelorn episode to impress a young woman and that he has not attended a meeting for many years. While I see that the evidence against Susan is also circumstantial she at least has a credible reason for wishing Lord Richard dead. There is no apparent reason to believe Mr McLeod wished any of the party ill.'

'Good God,' ejaculated Edward, 'if she's right, Fitzroy, we've been looking at this entirely wrong.'

Mr Fitzroy shrugged. 'I couldn't say.'

'I want to speak to this Susan,' said Mr Edward. 'I'll fetch her,' I said.

'No, you stay right here, young woman. I don't want you forewarning her.'

'I wouldn't do that!' I cried.

'Your face would do it for you,' snapped Edward. 'Fitzroy, pop your head out and see if there is some servant you can send for her.'

Susan arrived a few minutes later. She walked hesitantly into the room and, seeing the two gentlemen present, immediately cast her eyes down. Her fingers fidgeted with her apron and I could see sweat on her brow. I did not immediately take this as a sign of guilt, but it did remind me how most servants behaved in the presence of their so-called betters. No wonder the inhabitants of this house oscillated between thinking I was a heroine and a harlot. In their eyes, only a servant who was one or the other would behave as I had.

'I am Mr Edward, Susan. I need you to answer some questions truthfully. Can you do that?'

Susan nodded.

'Is it true you left wax on the hall staircase in the hope someone would be injured?'

138

Susan flicked me a sly look under her lashes and I realised I had misjudged her. She might be uncomfortable in the company of her betters, but she felt in no way compelled to reveal the truth. My heart sank. I was no closer to saving Rory. Susan opened her mouth and my worst fears were realised.

'Oh no, sir,' said Susan in a quiet, respectful voice. 'I couldn't find the right rags. Someone had moved them. I was only away a moment. What's she been saying?' She jerked her head towards me. 'She's never liked me.'

'Miss St John has been telling us about your father and his recent death,' said Mr Edward.

She swung round at me. 'You meddling cow! That's none of your business.' Then her face blanched. Her tongue nervously flickered around her lips. 'I'm sorry, Miss St John. I should never have spoke to you like that. It's been a trying time for all of us. I hope yous will accept my apology.'

She gave me a tiny curtsy.

'Of course, Susan, think nothing of it,' I said smiling. In my heart I was exulting. She had shown her true colours.

'You don't like Lord Richard, do you?' said Mr Edward with apparent sympathy.

'I does my job,' said Susan a little sullenly.

'But you don't like him?' persisted Mr Edward.

'It's not my place to like him,' protested Susan.

Mr Edward took a step closer, so he towered over her. 'I believe you hate him. Don't you?'

Susan said nothing.

'Don't you?' shouted Mr Edward, in a voice so loud I felt my bones shiver beneath my skin.

Something in Susan snapped and she spat, 'Would you like him if he turned your parents out of their home and left your children to starve?'

'But your husband? Couldn't he help you?' I asked blankly.

'Oh, you think you know everything, don't you? Miss high and mighty, but you don't know a thing. My John, my husband, he was killed on the estate. It was an accident, so the old master gave me a pension and let me keep my cottage. Lord Richard took that all away.'

'Come now, Susan, admit it,' said Mr Edward speaking now in a firm but strangely gentler tone. 'Is it not possible you might have hoped Lord Richard would slip on the stairs before you returned to finish them? Is it not true that you would not have greatly cared if this had happened? After all, as you say, this man had done his best to take everything from you.'

Susan bit her lip and twisted her hands together. I could see she was doing her best to force her feelings down and play the dutiful servant once more.

'I need you to be truthful if I am to help you,' said Mr Edward.

Susan said nothing. Her eyes darted back and forth between Mr Edward and me. She knew one of us was her enemy, but she was no longer sure which one.

'Would it not have struck you as a kind of divine justice if Lord Richard had fallen? The man whose ruthlessness, it is not too melodramatic to say, drove your father to his death? The man who has taken the bread from your children's mouths? Isn't

140

that what you wanted,' persisted Mr Edward. 'Justice? It is what we are all interested in here, in this room. We all want justice done.'

As they were meant to his words unlocked her anger. 'Justice? How am I going to get justice? I'm nothing compared to Lord Richard.'

'So you needed to take matters into your own hands. We all understand,' cajoled Mr Edward.

'The wains were starving. The old master looked the other way if we helped ourselves to a bit now and then.'

'Doubtless why he ran out of money,' muttered Fitzroy under his breath.

'Am I to understand, Susan, that you are confessing to thievery?' said Mr Edward.

Susan looked startled. 'Like you say, it was only justice. He took everything from me and I took a bit back.' She looked around at the faces in the room. 'Isn't that what this is about?'

'And the incident on the stairs?' asked Mr Edward.

'I'm not saying I did it deliberate.'

'But I think it is quite clear you wouldn't have minded if he had fallen. I am correct, am I not?' said Mr Edward.

Susan didn't answer.

Mr Edward reached behind him and pulled out a book. He got up and advanced on Susan. Suddenly he reached out and grabbed her wrist. He slammed her hand down onto the book. 'This is a bible, Susan. God will know if you lie. Did you wish Lord Richard harm?'

Susan struggled to pull her hand free.

'Answer me!' boomed Mr Edward.

141

'Sir!' I remonstrated.

'Answer me!' yelled Mr Edward again.

Susan collapsed at his feet sobbing. 'God help me but I did hope he would fall. I don't know what came over me. I've never done anything like it before. And he wasn't hurt. You can't arrest me.'

Mr Edward released her hand. He threw the book behind him onto a chair. 'But Mr Smith was, wasn't he?'

'What?' asked Susan wiping her tears away with the back of her hand.

'Those fatal cartridges you placed in the shooting bags. That was meant for Lord Richard, wasn't it?'

'You're away with the fairies. I dinna ken nothing about that!'

Mr Edward grabbed the girl by her arm and hauled her to her feet. 'You were quite right, Miss St John, to bring this matter to my attention. It is clear this woman is of murderous intent and that her scheme fell awry.'

'But I didn't! I didn't do anything to the shooting stuff. I wouldn't know how.'

'What did your husband do on the estate?' asked Mr Edward.

Susan hesitated.

'I can ask Lord Richard,' said Mr Edward.

'He was a gamekeeper,' said Susan in a tiny voice.

'And you would have me believe you do not know how a shotgun operates? You doubtless know better than the gentlemen themselves.'

'Give me the bible,' cried Susan. 'I'll swear on it. I'll swear I didn't harm anyone.'

142

'I have no doubt you would,' said Mr Edward. 'Any woman would perjure herself to stay with her children.'

'Oh God, the wains! My old mother! Who will look after them?'

'Very affecting,' said Mr Edward. 'It is a great pity you did not think of their welfare before.'

'What are you going to do with me?' cried Susan.

'You and Mr McLeod will exchange places. When the drive is rebuilt you will be taken away and tried for murder.'

'No!' cried Susan. Her knees buckled underneath her. I rushed forward to help, but Mr Edward had already roughly caught her up.

'I can manage, Miss St John,' he said coldly.

'But you can't,' I said breathlessly. 'You can't do this. The case against her is only circumstantial.'

'Thanks to you,' said Mr Edward, 'it is far more convincing than the case I had against Mr McLeod. You should be pleased, Miss St John. The household is about to regain a butler. I would say you have traded up.'

Chapter Eight

A Surfeit of Intruders and Suspects

'But he isn't even giving her a chance!' I cried as the door closed behind Mr Edward and the unfortunate Susan.

Mr Fitzroy rose and collected the book Mr Edward had discarded. 'Plato. If I didn't know better I would suspect Mr Edward has a sense of humour.'

'How can you make jokes at a time like this?' I demanded.

'It really *is* Plato,' said Mr Fitzroy. He held the book up so I could see the title.

'You know that is not what I meant!'

'My dear Miss St John, you have got exactly what you wanted. McLeod is exonerated and Susan is held culpable.'

'But she denied it!'

'As Mr Edward said, no woman is going to admit to a charge that makes her children orphans.'

'Oh dear God,' I said.

'Really, Miss St John, you should take more care in deciding what outcome you desire before you act.'

'Oh stop calling me by that ridiculous name,' I snapped and to my horror burst into tears. I buried my face in my hands and sobbed.

I was surprised when Mr Fitzroy took me by the elbow and steered me gently into a seat. He pressed a handkerchief on me and waited for my distress to subside.

'If it's any consolation, I don't believe she did it either,' he said.

'Then why?'

Mr Fitzroy shrugged. 'Locking up the butler wasn't getting us any nearer to finding the real killer.'

'You're trying to get the murderer to incriminate themselves? How?'

'It's a messy situation,' said Fitzroy, 'which currently you are significantly contributing to muddying.'

'I am only trying to do what is right.'

'If Mr Smith was the intended victim, then I will be doing all in my power to bring his killer to justice.'

'But not if it was *Lord Richard* who was the intended victim?'

Mr Fitzroy yawned. 'Provincial murder isn't one of my interests. Besides, Lord Richard remains alive and not in any apparent danger.'

I frowned. 'Were you particularly close to Mr Smith? You weren't at school with the others, were you?'

Mr Fitzroy stood up. 'If you're recovered, Euphemia, I am sure Mr McLeod will be eager to see you.' He paused and gave me a wry smile. 'To be updated about the household affairs, naturally.'

'Are you being deliberately mysterious, sir, or do you feel I am asking questions beyond my station?'

'Not beyond your station, my dear Miss Martins, but most definitely out of your league.'

'Sir, that is most ungentlemanly!'

'I have repeatedly told you, Euphemia, that I am no gentleman,' said Mr Fitzroy calmly.

'At least, sir, let us pool our resources. Previously, you encouraged me to investigate with your guidance...'

'No.'

'No?'

'Do not make me regret further taking you into my confidence.' There was real menace in his eyes. 'That would be unfortunate for us both.'

'But I know nothing about you.'

'I strongly advise we keep it that way,' said Fitzroy and threw open the door for me.

Realisation dawned on me. 'You believe, like Bertram, that this murder is one of international significance. You're a...'

Mr Fitzroy placed a finger suddenly against my lips. The speed at which he moved towards me made me fear he was going to strike me, but his finger against my flesh was quite gentle. He brought his face close to mine and whispered, 'Keep your foolish imaginings to yourself.'

I considered biting him, but that soft voice was more intimidating than any of the Staplefords' blusterings.

'Very wise,' said the hateful Mr Fitzroy. He stepped back and placed his hand on the door. He gestured smoothly for me to precede him and I did, hurrying away as fast as my pride would allow.

In the kitchen I came across a delighted Rory.

'It's good to see you, lass,' he cried, grabbing my hands. 'I believe it's you I have to thank for my liberty.'

I blushed and glanced around at the interested faces of Jock, Merry, Willie and several other staff, who it suddenly seemed needed to be in the kitchen at this hour. 'Should you not all be making the final preparations for dinner?' I asked. 'Is the staff supper being served before or afterwards, Jock? Really, I am away for a short time and you all become lax and inattentive to your duties.'

'Merry said you were leaving,' said Willie.

'Euphemia, is this true?' asked Rory.

'I am happy to say, it is not. There was a slight misunderstanding, but matters have now been arranged satisfactorily. Merry, Willie, I need you to check on the dining room. The gentlemen will be dining formally downstairs tonight. I need to know the settings and room are perfect. Jock, you will have to save the staff supper till later.' I looked at the other male servants, some of whom were valets, 'And you, gentlemen, need to remind your employers of tonight's formal meal. They have all of them returned quite muddy and I imagine will be in need of your aid. Mr McLeod, if you would be so good as to accompany me to my parlour, we can discuss what has happened in your absence.'

'I'm to keep my job then?'

'Certainly,' I said with authority. I looked around at the stunned sea of faces. 'The rest of you kindly get on with your business. Now!'

In the quiet of my parlour I passed Rory a whisky that I had requisitioned for him. 'I think it is the very least Lord Richard can do,' I said with a smile. I had a smaller glass for myself. I am not used to strong liquor, but this had been a most difficult day.

'Aye,' said Rory. 'I'm inclined to agree.' He took a mouthful and savoured it. It was the very best the house had to offer and it appeared to agree with him. 'It's a fine thing to be out of that pantry, but I'm gey sorry Susan will be the one taking my place. I'd never have thought it was a lassie who did this.'

I sipped at my own glass. The amber liquid glided over my tongue tasting of honey, heather and something sharper I couldn't identify. It settled warmly in my stomach. It was wonderful. No wonder the gentlemen drank this every evening. I took another sip.

'She didn't do it,' I said firmly. 'Investigations are continuing. Besides, the drive was washed away. The men were out again this afternoon shoring it up, but it will take more work to allow the passage of vehicles. Does it always rain in August in Scotland?'

'Not that often,' said Rory thoughtfully. 'I mean, there's always a bit of rain hanging around, but you lot do seem to have brought a fair squall up from the south.'

'You were with us!'

'Aye, but I was only visiting. This land is my home.'

'Will you continue working for the Staplefords?'

Rory shrugged. 'To be honest I'd rather not, but beggars can't be choosers and I don't have enough experience to get the kind of position I have here elsewhere.' He scratched his chin. 'If you see what I mean.'

'Certainly,' I said. 'And who is to say any other household would be less difficult?'

'I'd hope there might be less *murders*,' he said with a wry smile. 'What will happen to Susan? I know you said she was innocent, but that Mr Edward seemed very determined that she was guilty. I don't like to think of a woman locked up.'

'Or being hanged,' I said.

'Will it go that far, do you think?'

'Someone will be punished for this. I only hope it is the right person.'

'Us and them,' said Rory meaningfully.

'It's all so confusing,' I said with a grimace of annoyance. 'No one is sure if the intended victim was Mr Smith. He might have been given the bag with the wrong cartridges by accident. But he's Korean, or half-Korean, and Mr Bertram thinks that has something to do with it. That it's a political murder. I think Mr Fitzroy is a spy!'

Rory leaned over and took the almost empty glass from my hand. 'I think you'd better finish this later,' he said. 'I need to go and brush up to serve at dinner and you need to take it easy. You deserve a rest. I'll cover for you.' He lifted my feet onto a stool and threw a cover over me.

'I am not drunk,' I protested.

'No, just a little under the influence,' said Rory with a grin. 'Spies, indeed!'

'We should investigate,' I said. 'We need to help Susan.'

'No,' said Rory firmly. 'We should keep out of

149

it and do our jobs. Right now you need to rest.'

'It has all been most exhausting,' I said. 'Perhaps I will close my eyes for a few minutes.'

'Good idea,' said Rory. He closed the door softly behind him. My eyelids felt remarkably heavy, so I let them close. I told myself I would think more clearly about the puzzle I had to entangle if I shut out the world.

I am not entirely sure what happened, but I opened my eyes to a knock at my door. Merry tripped in. 'I kept a bit of supper back in the range, but if you want it before it all dries out you should come now. Unless you'd rather eat in here?'

I sat up rubbing my eyes. 'Is dinner over?' I asked blearily.

'Long over,' said Merry with a laugh. 'Mr McLeod said to leave you be, as you'd had a very hard day. Is that whisky I smell? You're not turning all Mrs Wilson on us, are you? Not that the Staplefords aren't enough to drive anyone to drink.'

I stood up brushing down my skirt. 'I had a small whisky with Mr McLeod to celebrate his release. I must have been more tired than I realised.'

'Of course,' said Merry, grinning.

'If the staff think I am lying in an inebriated stupor I had better come into the kitchen to disprove any gossip.'

'If you think you can walk straight,' muttered Merry.

'I heard that! I am quite fine!' I said making my way to the door. 'How is Susan?'

Merry's happy face fell. 'She's in the pantry. I heard her sobbing earlier. Do you really think she did it?'

'I don't know. She's admitted to leaving polish on the stairs in the hope of causing an accident.'

'I've felt like that more than once myself,' said Merry.

'Sssh!' Our pace had slowed as we talked, but I could feel the hairs rising on the back of my neck. I looked behind, but could see no one.

Merry stopped and leant against the passage wall. She looked up and down into the gloom. 'They've all gone,' she said. 'The locals have gone home and the rest are away to their own rooms. It's just us.'

'Hmm,' I said thoughtfully. 'Her husband was a gamekeeper, so it's believable she knew how to sabotage a gun. But getting the wrong cartridges to put in the bags would require preparation rather than an instant's madness.'

'Where would she get them?'

'I don't know. Although,' I admitted slowly, 'it's possible they were already here. Apparently they're the ones Miss Richenda would have used if she'd come up.'

'Who packed up that stuff?'

'I saw Rory with the guns, but I don't know about the ammunition. It might have been Lord Richard.'

'It would be like him to bring the whole lot rather than sort it all out.'

'Perhaps,' I said, 'he's not a very thorough man. But that would mean Susan could have come across the cartridges when she was helping you.'

'I didn't see her open any of the ammunition bags.'

'But if she didn't, how did it get in there?'

'Who packed them?' asked Merry.

'It must have been either Rory or the new gamekeeper.'

'Lots of people were around those bags,' said Merry. 'It could have been anyone.'

'Or it could have been a tragic accident. Someone made an error in packing and...'

'You should go and eat what's left of your supper,' said Merry. 'The whole thing seems clear as mud to me.'

'With this amount of rain it would have to be,' I said smiling.

'What?' asked Merry warily. 'Are you making fun of me?'

'You know what,' I said decidedly, 'talking to you has definitely helped. I need to go out to the shoot and see if there was any way someone could have tampered with the bags on the site. It's much more likely that this murder was done by one of the guests or the Staplefords. Servants may hate their masters, but they know if anything happens to one of the so-called "nobs" life is only going to get worse for them.'

'Euphemia, what are you like? It's pitch black out there.'

'I'll go tomorrow, around dawn, before anyone is up and around. If I'm actually at the scene of the crime I might get some more ideas.'

'You're creepy sometimes, you know that?'

'I want to help Susan,' I said flatly. 'It's my fault she's been accused and there's no more of a case against her than there was against Rory.'

'If you ask me, I think...'

It was at this point I noticed a portion of

shadow detach itself from the wall and move off.

'There's someone there,' I cried. 'They must have heard every word we said!'

'Where?' asked Merry peering into the gloom. 'Hey, wait, Euphemia, don't go following a murderer, for the love of God!'

But I didn't stay to listen. I crept quickly along the passageway. There was very little light, only the occasional pale streak of moonlight, so I didn't risk running. It would do no one any good if I broke my neck in the dark. I followed as fast as I dared. Within moments I reached a junction; looking right and left, I could see no trace of my supposed intruder. Behind me, Merry clattered into a bucket in the dark. She swore loudly. I knew there was very little chance of following the intruder. But as my eyes grew accustomed to the dark, I saw a faint trace of light off to the left. It was coming from the second pantry where Susan was being held! Someone was trying to free her – or worse. It occurred to me in a sudden flash that if Susan were silenced, then the case could be closed and the real murderer would get away. Despite the darkness I broke into a run.

'This way, Merry!' I yelled.

The door to the second pantry was wide open. A pale yellow light from an oil lamp washed out into the passage. My ears could make out a low murmur of conversation. The escape was not yet complete. I rushed up to the door and stopped on the threshold stunned by what I saw. Behind me I heard Merry's boots clatter to a halt. 'Oh lor',' I heard her say softly.

In the pantry, seated on the stool, was a weeping Susan. Her hair hung about her face and it was clear she had been distraught for some time. There was nothing unexpected about the sight of her. It was Mr Bertram kneeling at her feet, her small hands enfolded in his larger ones, that took my breath away. He turned his head at our noisy arrival, but only nodded curtly before transferring his attention back to Susan.

'I assure you, Susan, no matter what happens I will ensure your family are taken care of.'

Tears spilled onto his hands from her face. 'But sir, my wains, my poor wee mites. I didn't do it, sir, I didn't do it!'

Mr Bertram untangled one of his hands and gently pushed Susan's hair back from her face. 'I know, Susan, and I will not rest until you are free. You have to trust me. It will be all right.'

'I think, sir,' I said through gritted teeth. 'It would be better for all concerned if you left now. This door must be closed and locked.'

'Have you no heart, Euphemia?' said Mr Bertram.

'I am only suggesting you follow the advice you gave to me earlier, sir, and leave this to the authorities. I do not think neither Mr Edward nor Lord Richard would be pleased at this interference.'

Mr Bertram patted Susan's hand, disengaged himself and stood up. 'Euphemia is right. My being here compromises us both, but I will keep my word to you and I will see you free. Please, keep the lamp.'

He came out and closed the door on the weeping woman. He turned the key in the lock and handed it to me. 'Satisfied?' he said quietly.

154

Behind me I heard Merry slope off.

'I cannot understand your behaviour,' I said in a low voice. 'You tell me not to meddle in these affairs and then I find you here, in the middle of the night, colluding with the accused!'

'It is your fault she is in there,' said Mr Bertram. 'If you had let things be...'

'Then Rory would have been hanged for a crime he did not commit.'

'So when it's *Rory*, you take an interest?' asked Mr Bertram, placing what I felt was rather unnecessary emphasis on the butler's name.

'He was innocent,' I said hotly. 'The case against him was weak and circumstantial.'

'And the case against Susan isn't?' snapped Mr Bertram. 'Are you sure Mr McLeod is the innocent you think him or are your personal prejudices swaying you? For crying out loud, the man is a communist!'

'He has explained that,' I said with as much dignity as I could muster. 'It was a youthful indiscretion.'

'Euphemia, when will you understand this is a political killing? You are out of your depth here! You've let that man take you in!'

'I take it you are now an expert on political killings?'

Mr Bertram ran his fingers through his hair. 'You are enough to drive a saint to distraction.' He lowered his hands to his side and grasped them into fists. 'When I was Smith's fag at school I learned that his father was a member of the now-exiled Korean government. You need to stop meddling, Euphemia, before anyone else is hurt.'

'Anyone else?'

'Until the real killer is found, Smithy's parents, and younger brother, and sister are all in danger. All you have done is confuse and endanger innocents. I warned you about meddling.'

'And now you're going to step in and save the day?' Even to my own ears this sounded petulant.

'I bid you goodnight, Miss St John,' said Mr Bertram and walked off.

I stood in the darkness for a short while struggling with my emotions. I was so angry I literally could not see the passage in front of me. How dare he! How dare he speak to me like that! And to be so intimate with a domestic! If I had not arrived, who knows what would have happened? Mr Bertram and I had been through a lot together, but he had never looked at me as tenderly as he had regarded Susan. Why, he had even stroked her face. I pounded my fist against the wall. It hurt a lot. The pain brought me to my senses. I became aware of Susan still quietly sobbing behind the door. For the first time I heard her for what she was, a mother sobbing for her children. 'Dear God,' I breathed. 'What have I done?'

For once the darkness held no fear for me. I was too tormented by my own inner demons to fear insubstantial ones without. I made my way towards my chamber thinking only of the words of Mr Fitzroy and Mr Bertram that I was out of my depth. Could my instincts have led me wrong? Could it be Rory really was guilty? I paused on the stair, conjuring up his face in my mind's eye. His luminous eyes could certainly reflect sternness and discipline, but there was also warmth

156

and laughter within them. In the short time I had known him I had felt I had found a friend. Could I have been misled by my loneliness? Could I have lost my head over a man with a handsome face and a tall, inviting shoulder I was so eager to lean upon? I gave myself a little shake and walked on up the stairs. No, I was merely tired and over-wrought. There was no possibility of friendship between Rory and I – our stations were far too dissimilar. But does my heart understand the necessities of rank? whispered a small voice at the back of my mind.

Merry was already abed and snoring loudly. I undressed without light. Since my entrance into service I had become quite adept at handling buttons in the dark. I pushed a chair against the door. I would never grow used to having an un-lockable sleeping chamber and slid under the covers, but sleep was far from my weary grasp. I turned the situation over and over in my mind, but every time I thought through the sequence of events, I became more confused. I felt as if my brain would rattle to pieces. The feeling was so intense I fancied I could actually hear the noise of my poor mind disintegrating.

It was then I realised there really *was* a rattling noise. I turned my head slowly, not wishing to see what I feared I must. Helpfully, a shaft of moon-light broke across the room and I saw the door handle, wedged tight on the top of the chair, was twisting slowly back and forth.

I threw back the covers and hurried across to Merry's bed. 'Merry,' I hissed, shaking her. 'Wake up! Someone is trying to get in!'

'Hermpf? What?' said Merry sleepily.

I lowered my lip to her ear and whispered forcefully. 'Someone is trying to break into our room!'

The chair moved slightly, scraping along the ground with an eerie squeak. Merry sat up in bed. Her eyes fixed on the door handle. It twisted back and forth. Whoever was trying the door wasn't prepared to give up easily.

'The chair'll hold it,' said Merry quietly.

The chair slid a little farther.

'Not for long,' I said.

'Who do you think it is? Rory?' said Merry, suppressing a giggle at the thought.

'I think it's the murderer,' I said softly. 'I think someone heard me say I was going up to the site tomorrow and they don't want me to go.'

'Oh lor',' said Merry.

'What shall we do?' I said looking her in the eye and willing her to give the right response. 'Do we cower in our beds and hope the chair holds or do we expose the man and save Susan?'

In answer Merry grabbed the candlestick off her nightstand. I picked up mine. 'I reckon if we yank the door open and scream, it'll scare the life out of the bugger,' said Merry. 'If we both bash him at the same time, that should do it.'

I nodded. We padded over to the door. I placed my hand on the back of the chair. It had almost slid entirely free. The door handle still turned. I looked at Merry. 'Ready?' I asked. Merry nodded. 'On three,' I said. 'One, two, three!'

We both inhaled deeply as I thrust the chair aside. Merry flung open the door. We rushed forth, screaming with our candlesticks aloft and met only empty air.

Whoever had been there had fled.

'They must have overheard us,' I said.

'Two stout-hearted maids armed with candle-sticks and powerful screams are not to be taken lightly,' joked Merry. Even in the dark, I could see she was trembling with fear despite her brave words.

I closed the door. 'That's as may be, but it gets us no nearer to solving this mystery. I must continue with my plan.'

'But they might have heard you!' exclaimed Merry.

'It might also have been Baggy Tipton looking for female companionship.'

'He wouldn't!' exclaimed Merry. 'He's a wimpy little man.'

'Brandy is a great disinhibitor,' I said.

'But what if it wasn't?' persisted Merry.

'I'm going. Whatever the risk. I have to,' I said resolutely. 'And don't you breathe a word to any-one!'

Chapter Nine

A Meeting in the Glen

I slept little that night. We wedged the chair more tightly in place and shored it up with a night-stand, but I think neither Merry nor I were able to give ourselves over to slumber after what had occurred. I rose at first light.

The sun was still rising when I let myself out of the back door. No one else was stirring and I found myself walking along a wet, leafy lane with only the morning cries of hidden birds for company.

This side of the house led by a series of interconnected narrow lanes and pathways to the estate cottages. The drive was still impassable by carriage and I had not fancied my chances of scrambling along it even in a very strong pair of boots. My plan was to walk almost to the second set of cottages, where Susan lodged, but to break off and head up the hill at this point. I hoped I could then make my way across country to the shooting site. I anticipated a long, difficult and muddy climb, but no worse than I had attempted when I lived in Sweetfield. I could only hope my time at Stapleford Hall had not sapped my strength. Considering the long hours and hard work Mrs Wilson put me to, I had every reason to believe myself fitter than ever.

However, fit though I might be, an hour later I was beginning to fear that Scottish mud and steep inclines would triumph over my intentions. It had also begun to drizzle lightly and all in all I was feeling much less enthusiastic about my whole plan. I doubted my ability, my skills, my sense and was a miserable bedraggled creature when the lane I was currently traversing opened up and revealed a crossroads. I sat down on the edge of the small mile-marker and enjoyed a very necessary rest.

The rain pattered off the leaves and the air was

full of the scent of earth. I took a moment to focus on my surroundings and remind myself of the peace that is to be found in nature. It is not something I have had enough occasion to do while working for the Staplefords. The glory of the natural world worked its magic upon me and, in a short while, I found myself confident of success. Justice was on my side and Pa had always taught me that, with the aid of quick wits, a stout heart and determination, good and right would always prevail. Of course, it was his vocation to believe such things.

I took my notebook out of my pocket and discovered that the waxed paper I had used to protect it from the rain had done its job well. I closed my eyes and quickly sketched what I remembered of the shooting site and the position of the pegs. I knew where Mr Smith had fallen and could well recall the grouping of gentlemen Rory and I had seen near the body. I hoped a return to the scene might correct any errors and perhaps allow my shocked mind to remember any slight detail that would make a difference. I certainly intended to walk the very journey the cartridge bags had gone and by working my way through the events in proper sequence I might yet discover something that drew suspicion away from Susan.

I was quite lost in thought when I heard the clip-clop of hooves. Looking up I saw a small trap coming along the lane. A man in a large hat and waxed coat was driving. There appeared to be logs and other materials piled behind him in what had obviously once been meant for transporting people. I was unsure of local etiquette, but I stood up to greet him as he passed.

'It's a wet day for a walk,' he said in a thick accent. Under the wide brim I looked up into a pair of friendly hazel eyes, set all about with the lines of many years. 'Where ye off to, lass? Can I give yous a ride?'

As I have sadly remarked before, lying comes more easily to me now I work for the Staplefords. 'One of the gentlemen at the lodge lost an expensive, engraved hipflask at the shoot and I am sent to search for it.'

The old man made a hawking noise in his throat and spat into the road. I flinched although his aim was true and it landed far from me. 'Them calls themselves gentlemen and make more a fuss of a piece of trumpery than a life!'

'I believe it was his father's and may have some sentimental attachment, but I agree it is nothing compared to what has happened. But I'm only a servant.'

'You don't sound like one,' he said suspiciously.

'My father was a vicar – a minister, I believe you call them here – and when he died my mother could not support me or herself, so I entered service.'

'I'm sure he is enjoying the Lord's reward,' said the man with unexpected kindness that brought tears to my eyes. 'Hop up, lass. I'm heading to the upper woods and I can drop you close to the site. I won't be able to bring you back though. I'll be working the woods for the rest of the day.'

I climbed up the side of the trap and sat beside him. 'This is very welcome, sir,' I said. 'I'm sure the walk down will be easier than the walk up. I grew up in the country, but it was not as wild or as beautiful as here.'

The man clicked his tongue and the horse moved off. 'It's a grand country, but a cruel mistress,' he said. 'I'm Donal Strachan. I'm gamekeeper on the estate.'

'You must have worked with Susan's husband,' I blurted out.

'Aye, a grand man. There was more than enough work for two. Still is. Yer ken Susan?'

'A little. Well, enough not to believe she did what they say she did.'

'She's a passionate lass. Aye-ways was. If it had been the new master that had died I might have credited it, but this Mr Smith that no one has ever heard of? It makes no sense.'

'She'd have known then about the danger of a wrong cartridge. I don't really understand it myself.'

'Aye. More so than most of the gentlemen, I reckon. Lachlan, that's her husband, and I used to make our own loads. Fill the cartridges ourselves. It's a dirty job, but cheaper by far than buying them from some fancy gunmaker. We also tend to be given the old guns, so you have to know the risks. A shotgun is a powerful weapon. The blast it gives out...' He looked at me. 'Do you know what is in a cartridge?'

'No, I don't.'

'I suppose your father being a man of God wasn't prone to shooting the Lord's beasts.'

'No,' I said simply, hoping he would continue.

'Well, inside one of those wee cylinders is the

163

exploding powder like you'd get in any gun, a wad that holds the shot together and lots and lots of wee metal balls. Think of them like tiny cannon-balls and you'll not go far wrong. When the gun is fired, the powder ignites and pushes the wad and the shot along the barrel. The wad is needed to hold the shot close, so it can fly together for longer. Otherwise you'd get the effect of an old blunderbuss. The shot flies true and gradually spreads into a cloud form as it travels through the air. A good close shot peppers your target with holes. If it's close enough, it punches a hole straight through. Farther off and a few pellets will catch this and that. That's one of the reasons you need a good dog at a shoot so it will find the wounded, as well as the slaughtered birds, so they can be put out of their misery.'

I felt slightly sick, but I managed to ask, 'What happens to the wad?'

'Smart lassie,' said the man approvingly. 'It flies out the chamber, falling away from the shot.'

'It wouldn't be the wad stuck in the chamber that caused the gun to go off?'

'Unlikely.'

'I don't understand what happened then.'

'From what I heard it sounds like someone put in a 20 bore cartridge. That's a smaller cartridge – the kind a lady's gun uses – instead of a 12 bore. Despite the numbers, that's a bigger cart-ridge.'

'Wouldn't it just fall out of the barrel?'

'Nay, bless you lass. Would that it could. It drops down a wee bit, so when the gun is fired the cap doesn't ignite. It just lodges in the chamber, but

164

far enough down that it's easy enough to put another cartridge in on top. And when the second cartridge is fired the chamber is blocked, so the explosion doesn't go out along the barrel but back towards the head of the man holding the gun.'

'So his head receives all the full force of the blast.'

'That's about the size of it,' said Donal. 'Sometimes the wad from a home-load lodges in the barrel or someone takes a wrong cartridge. That's why you'll see a man who knows about guns check his barrels after each shot. But it should never happen with the posh stuff your master buys.'

'They wouldn't have been doing that on the 12th, would they?'

'Nay, lass. The competition to get the most birds and the bloodlust that gets on them'll drive the sense out of most gentlemen.'

'I doubt they realise the risk.'

'Probably not,' the man admitted. 'That's one of the reasons the loader is there. He loads a second gun between shots and passes the loaded gun to the shooter. He takes back the gun that's been used and checks it. Folks think his job, and the second gun, are just about making the gentleman shoot faster, but it's as much about safety.'

'Could a bought cartridge not be faulty too? Badly made?'

'I'd like to think so, lass. But I heard they found a mixture of cartridges on him.' The man sighed. 'He didn't have a loader with him, did he?'

'No, he'd been called away.'

'It's a shame that. A good loader would have spotted it.' He smiled slightly. 'A bad loader

165

would have had his head shot off too.'

'It would have killed him?' I asked my voice catching in my throat.

'Anyone standing next to a gun that explodes is a dead man.'

'But none of the other shooters were injured.'

'I can tell you've never seen a shoot up close,' said Donal. 'It works like this. The Glorious Twelfth is a competitive time. The guns, the gentlemen, insist on knowing their own tally. So pegs – shooting spots – are set up across the hill, each far enough apart from the other so the kills will be easily attributed.'

'They can't all be equally good places. Who decides who shoots where?' I asked.

'It's done by lot right before they start shooting.'

'It's all very confusing.'

'A shoot can be a confusing place and it grieves me to say it, but Susan would ken that.'

'You think she changed the ammunition, don't you?'

'If she did, she put it in the wrong bag,' said Donal. 'The other person I'd be looking at close, if it were up to me, is his loader. It's not usual for a loader to walk off, especially not on the Glorious Twelfth.'

My stomach turned over. Could I have got everything very wrong and let free the real killer?

My thoughts silenced me. Donal drove on and up the mountainside. Here the light rain became more mist-like. Although it was more than clear enough to drive by, there was a smudged whitish taint to everything. I was not looking forward to

166

crossing the fields, but when Donal pulled up to let me down I had no choice. I thanked him politely and waved until the trap was out of sight.

The echo of hooves and the rattle of the trap faded into the distance. I have always enjoyed walking in the country, but now, whether it was the dimness of the weather, the cold that was beginning to seep into my bones despite the shawl I had wrapped around myself, or simply the grim nature of my self-imposed task, I do not know, but I had the strangest feeling I was not alone.

Unlike my brother, Little Joe, I am not given to fancying myself in the presence of spirits, but as I picked my way across the field towards the shooting site, I could not but think I would far rather encounter the ghost of the kindly Mr Smith than some dark stranger rising out of the mist.

I reached the shooting site without incident. I found shelter beneath some trees. There was even a dry stretch of bark to lean against. I drew out my pocketbook and turned to my earlier sketch to check what I remembered from the terrible day. I was able to position Mr Smith accurately and, after some thought, draw in the situation of several of the gentlemen. It did not tell me who had been at which peg, but it gave some indication of nearness presuming all the men including the killer had responded in similar time to the explosion. One of the risks the killer would have had to have taken was that he might end up close to the exploding gun. I could think of no way that the taking of lots for the pegs could have been arranged.

I reasoned if I were the killer I would have been careful to react in as innocent a manner as possible, which would include appearing to hasten to Smith's aid even though I would have had good reason to know he was already dead.

Tipton and Rory had arrived after the explosion, but that did not matter. The cartridge could have been placed at any time in the bag. Of course, if Rory was the killer, then he would have had to ensure the cartridge was not used while he was present. I went back over the events in my mind. Could the bag have been tampered with at lunch?

I walked slowly back to the lunch site. I was rapidly coming to the conclusion that a great many people would have had the opportunity to tamper with the bag. I could not precisely recall where the bags had been placed during luncheon, but the gentlemen had certainly not sat down with them still around their waists.

I stopped, struck by a sudden thought. Why was I presuming the gentlemen were wearing the cartridge bags? I had paid little attention to their shooting attire. Might they not have been carried by the loaders? My head spun. There was so much I didn't know. Mr Smith had both a bag and cartridges in his pocket. There was something in that, but I couldn't grasp the thought.

Had Mr Edward questioned the gentlemen about all of this? I could only presume he had. All my doubts washed over me again. Last time I had been involved with investigating a murder I had not had to think about where the weapon had come from. Instead I had concentrated solely on the personalities of the people involved. I had pursued my train of thought with such vigour that while tracking down clues I had attracted the attention of the murderer and in one case achieved a confession. However, the man who had confessed to me bore me no ill will and had been driven to his crime by deeds that would have tried the saintliest of men. I had no illusions any of the guests at the lodge were saints.

Mr Bertram and Mr Fitzroy were right. I was out of my depth. I was lacking the kind of mind that focuses well on the tiny details of movement. My only successes were down to an understanding of the personalities involved and I barely knew the names of the guests here.

But then, my inner voice prompted, you had been in the presence of the Staplefords for less than a day when you discovered a corpse and there were still leads for you to follow.

I was now at the luncheon site. I managed to find a dry spot under a tree with protruding roots and made myself an uncomfortable seat.

The male sex is often a mystery to me, but I could not conceive of the kind of man who calmly dines with another he intends to kill shortly afterwards. Would there not have been some sign of this in his behaviour at lunch?

I tried to recall who had been eager to return to the shoot and who reluctant. I remembered first that Rory had repeatedly urged Lord Richard to return and even attempted to withhold the wine. I knew in my heart I wanted Rory to be innocent and I could imagine he was doing no more than attempting to prevent drunken men from handling dangerous weapons. However, he had also forced a confrontation with his master, and few servants as keen to preserve their positions, as he claimed to be, would have done that.

I remembered too that Muller had been eager to return. Mr Bertram had been uncomfortable throughout the meal, but then he had displayed a high level of discomfort since the guests had first arrived. I carried within me the sad disappointment of knowing he followed on his brother's coattails in search of material wealth. Had I sadly misjudged him? I did not think him a murderer, but I knew from bitter experience he was capable of looking the other way, whatever he had said to the weeping Susan.

Of the others, I recalled Tipton had wanted to stay on and drink. Could it be he had intended inebriation to be a reason why he could not return to the shoot and the potential danger of an exploding gun? Or was he simply looking for an excuse to remain behind and accost me? Had that always been his intention or had the drink loosened his morals?

McGillvary had attempted diplomacy and suggested Tipton should be supplied with his drink. He had appeared to have had no preference either way as to returning to the shooting.

I did recall that when Mr Smith had exited the table early, as I had interpreted it, to escape the increasingly uncomfortable situation, Fitzroy had immediately decided to accompany him. Could his intention have been to plant the wrong cartridges then on Mr Smith? Had he been deliberately misleading me all along?

Rory and Tipton were the two who struck me as behaving most oddly. Muller had no issue with returning to the shoot and could thus be ruled out of expecting any danger and by extension of the murder.

I would very much have liked to have had cause to suspect Lord Richard, but he had been no other than his usual, blustering, bullying self.

It was true that many people had opportunity to tamper with the bags, but those with the easiest access and opportunity were Rory and Fitzroy. Although Rory's opportunity was greater.

It struck me also that this murderer must be a person of nerve. There had been more than one false cartridge found on Mr Smith. The only conclusion I drew from this was that the murderer did not mind it being known as murder. I pushed my damp hair away from my furrowed brow. This lent credence to Mr Bertram's theory that it was politically motivated. Possibly even a warning to others. Certainly it ruled out Susan, who – even in the height of her passion – would have not wanted the crime detected for the sake of her children.

No, the man who had perpetrated this crime was as cool-headed as he was intelligent. He was confident the evidence was so tangled he would never be exposed and he was content to sit and watch us run around like headless chickens. My stomach turned over as I realised the inappropriateness of my metaphor.

The mist was clearing. The site before me no longer bore any sign of the events of the 12th. I leaned back against the gnarly tree and closed my eyes. The only conclusions I had been able to draw were unwelcome ones and also ones that were difficult to substantiate.

'Euphemia!'

My eyes snapped open to see Rory running across the field towards me. I blinked twice thinking I must be dreaming.

'Thank goodness I've found you. Merry told me of your plan. I was worried for your safety.'

His bright blond locks had been darkened by the rain, but not so his green eyes that smiled so warmly down at me. I felt a cold shiver run down my spine. I could not think of any circumstance that would induce Merry to reveal our plan.

'She told you?' I asked.

'Aye,' said Rory. 'Lord Richard was looking for you.'

'This early in the morning?'

'Aye. What's wrong, Euphemia?'

It was at this moment that Mr McGillvary broke into the clearing carrying a gun. 'Miss St John,' he cried. 'Step away from that man! Come to me!'

I rose.

Rory grabbed my arm. 'Euphemia, you can't believe it was me!'

I looked into his eyes and saw nothing but honesty and warmth. 'Did you check the cartridges in Smith's bag before the shoot?' I asked.

'Yes,' said Rory. 'I didn't check the man's pockets, but I checked all the ammunition before it went up to the site.'

'A pretty clear admission of guilt,' said McGillvary. 'Step away, Miss St John.'

'Why did you abandon your place as loader?' I asked.

'I saw the way Tipton had been looking at you at lunch. When he didn't join the others for the afternoon shoot, I became concerned for you.'

'And Smith didn't mind you leaving him?'

'I think he'd noticed the same thing. He told me not to worry, that he often shot without a loader. He scooped out some cartridges from the bag. Told me to leave it at his feet. He made some joke about needing fewer shots than the others.'

Finally my thoughts came into focus. 'What if,' I said slowly, 'the 12 bore cartridges were never in the bag? What if they were only ever in his pocket?'

'You mean he brought them himself?' asked Rory blankly. 'He was a skilled shooter. He'd never have made that kind of mistake.'

McGillvary met my level gaze. He said nothing. A slow smile spread across his face.

'No, Rory,' I said sadly. 'He didn't. It was done by the only man who asked for hand-warmers to keep his fingers nimble. The man who practises magic tricks for his nephew, who produced a flower from behind Susan's ear on his first day here. It was done by a man skilled in sleight of hand. Such a very small trick, to tip a cartridge or two into his friend's pocket.'

'Oh well done, Euphemia,' said McGillvary. 'I knew you were smarter than Edward. If anyone was going to figure it out it was going to be you.'

'You're the one who has been stalking me,' I said. 'You tried to get into my room last night. You were in the corridor. You tried to get to Rory

173

and then Susan before their innocence could be proven!'

'You have been so terribly difficult to get alone,' said Mr McGillvary, 'but now it seems I will be able to kill two birds with two shots and solve all my problems.'

He levelled his gun at us.

Chapter Ten

Of King and Country, Love and Jealousy

There was no chance of escape. McGillvary had come through the woods from the opposite side of the clearing. Rory had come from my left. That way the trees thinned out. This and the clearing itself could only be considered a killing ground. There was a tree pressing into my back, while behind me the trees and surrounding scrub were too dense to allow flight. There was no way to escape McGillvary without running in front of his gun.

'Why? Why did you kill him?' I asked frantically, trying to buy us more time. I had little expectation he would answer me, but he did. He still had that slow, satisfied smile plastered across his thin lips.

'You never suspected me, did you?'

'No,' I said still thinking furiously. 'How could you? He was your friend.'

'That was the beauty of it. I could get close to

him and no one thought anything of it.'

'But why?' I was running out of questions.

'Because someone asked me to, Euphemia. Someone who could put a number of advantages my way.'

'Chopsticks,' I said suddenly. 'Lord Richard said you dealt in chopsticks. You have business in the Far East, don't you? What happened? Did you run aground?'

McGillvary snarled and I realised I had hit the mark. 'It's none of your business. Enough talking. Let's get this over with.'

'You'll never get away with it!' I cried. 'You'll never be able to explain both our deaths! The roads are still out. You can't get away!'

'I won't need to,' said McGillvary smoothly. 'Unlike you, my dear Euphemia, I always have a plan.'

'She's right. You won't get away with this, McGillvary!' said Rory.

'Oh, I think I will,' he replied. 'You see, I shall say Euphemia told me of her plan to visit the site and, fearing for her life, I came after her, but sadly I was too late. You, McLeod, dastardly villain that you are, had already shot her. You turned the second barrel on me and, in self-defence, I shot you. I have another gun behind the tree which I shall discharge for verisimilitude after I have given you one barrel each from this gun.'

'That's a ridiculous tale,' I said. 'No one will believe you. I've already spoken to both Mr Bertram and Mr Edward about my suspicions.'

'But you never suspected me, did you?'

I tried to keep my expression level, but he saw

175

the truth in it. I had no idea how I would get out of this.

'They won't believe you,' I urged again.

McGillvary laughed. 'Let us see. You are a servant. He is a communist. And I am a gentleman. Who do you think they will believe?'

I realised he did intend to kill us. From what Donal Strachan had told me, running towards a shotgun would only ensure death. The tree was at my back. If Rory and I ran quickly in different directions one of us might get beyond the distance at which fatality was assured.

These thoughts flashed through my mind in an instant. There was no time for discussion. There was no time at all.

McGillvary slid the safety catch off. 'Now, which one of you shall I shoot first?'

I did not want to abandon Rory. Neither did I want to die like a coward. But above all I did not want to die at all. I prepared to run.

'I think I'll shoot the girl. You're a mouthy wench, my dear, and the world will be more peaceful for your absence.'

Looking into that long, dark barrel I felt my legs grow weak. McGillvary nestled the gun further into his shoulder and lowered his face to the gun. I had to run now, but where? Which way would give me the best chance? Any chance. I had to move now!

It was then that Rory thrust me aside and stood in my place. I fell to the ground. I had one last look at his determined face as he stood over me and then the gun fired. So close the sound was deafening. The smell of cordite filled the air.

Except Rory didn't fall. To his obvious aston-ishment and my own, he stood there perfectly intact. Then I saw understanding dawn on his face. He put out his hand and helped me up. It was only then I understood. McGillvary lay bleeding on the ground, his gun flung from him across the grass.

Mr Fitzroy emerged from the clearing, holding a smoking shotgun. He went forwards and calmly checked that life was extinguished. He broke his gun and put it on the grass. Then he did the same for the second gun.

'You were lucky that didn't go off,' he said con-versationally to Rory. 'That was a very brave and gentlemanly thing you did. Brave, but stupid.'

'How...' My brain was unable to finish the sentence.

Mr Fitzroy indicated the first gun. 'This?'

'Uh-huh,' I said. My tongue felt thick and leaden.

'McGillvary kindly left this behind the tree. Weren't you listening, Euphemia?'

'I was rather busy trying to think of how I might survive,' I said, finally finding my proper voice. 'And I don't think Rory was in the least bit stupid. He was terribly brave.' I took his arm and smiled up into his face. 'Thank you,' I said sincerely.

Rory blushed.

Mr Fitzroy sighed. 'How romantic and yet so shortsighted. There are worse things for a woman than being dead and with Mr McLeod out of the way there was no reason for McGillvary to keep his distance. I'd say shooting you first was an almost chivalrous act, Euphemia, except I know how very annoying you can be.'

'Sir, we are both extremely grateful, but I don't think there is any call to insult the lady.'

Fitzroy grinned. 'You don't know her very well, do you?' he said.

'Why are you here?' I asked. 'This isn't an easy place to find.'

'I think it's best if you take a leaf out of Mr McLeod's book and merely express your gratitude.' The smile was still on his face, but his eyes had hardened.

'You were watching McGillvary!' I said in a moment of realisation. 'How long had you suspected him?'

'In my line of work I find it is healthy to suspect everyone.'

'You *are* a spy!' I exclaimed. The glittering look he gave me frightened me almost as much as the gun barrels had earlier. 'I'm sorry,' I said quickly. 'I won't say that again.'

'I'd advise you not to,' said Mr Fitzroy, with a calm I found extremely unnerving. 'In fact, it would be better for all concerned if you both entirely forget today's events. I will need your word on that.'

'But we've seen a murder,' protested Rory. 'I'm grateful and all. You saved our lives, but you didn't even give the man the chance of laying down his gun.'

'Such chivalry,' muttered Mr Fitzroy. 'It really will get you killed. He would undoubtedly have fired on me first and then yourself, trusting he could finish Euphemia with his bare hands.'

'Aye, but is it not still murder?'

178

'It was an execution,' said Mr Fitzroy bluntly. 'Mr Edward will vouch I was merely doing my job.'

'Are you here to check out Lord Richard?' I asked.

'My dear girl, your wisest course of action would be to rid yourself of this incipient rampant curiosity. It is most unhealthy.'

'But we can't just leave him here,' said Rory.

'That is exactly what you must do,' said Fitzroy. 'The matter will be dealt with. I am leaving now. I suggest you make your own way back to the lodge. Mr Edward will no doubt help you overcome any lingering scruples.'

He tipped his cap to me, turned on his heel and strode away into the forest leaving McGillvary and the guns lying on the ground.

It took Rory and me some time to make our way back to the lodge. We encountered no one else. It was a difficult and muddy walk. Rory was kind and assiduous in helping me over the obstacles that lay in our way, but we said little to each other. It might have been supposed, with the departure of Fitzroy, we would discuss at length our fortunate escape, but in my mind lay many unanswered questions. At least some of these were questions that I felt frightened to pose.

I could see bewilderment in Rory's face. This was his first murder. It was my third and I suspected in some dark way this lessened my shock. The curious – I might say barely credible – speeches by Mr Fitzroy opened up more questions than it closed. Both of us, I had no doubt, had the imprint of this morning's events etched in our

179

minds for ever and yet neither of us understood what we had seen.

I had heard my father often say that angels came in many guises, but my heart told me Mr Fitzroy was no angel.

To my astonishment Mr Edward was waiting for us in the kitchen. He looked quite at home, sitting by the range-side, munching on a poached egg sandwich and, between mouthfuls, discussing football with Jock.

'Ah, the wanderers return,' he said, rising. 'If you would be so good as to accompany me to the library.'

Rory began to speak, but Mr Edward merely said, 'Not here,' and walked out of the kitchen.

I saw no option but to follow him. Rory fell into step behind me. Mr Edward took us into the library. He closed the door and gestured to us to be seated. He then poured us both a whisky. I had less difficulty with this than Rory, who was clearly unused to such blurring of the social lines.

'Lord Richard,' said Rory helplessly holding up his glass.

'All matters will be taken care of,' said Mr Edward calmingly. 'However, I am afraid I shall have to ask you to report on what transpired on the hill. I trust the fact Mr Fitzroy is not accompanying you is not an indicator he was injured?'

'Fitzroy, no,' said Rory and swallowed a large mouthful of whisky. 'But McGillvary is dead.'

'Was Mr Fitzroy responsible for his demise?'

'Fitzroy, yes,' said Rory swallowing some more.

Mr Edward turned his attention to me. 'Miss St John, you have never had a problem expressing

180

yourself. Perhaps you might tell me what transpired?'

I stared into the fire and shivered.

'Drink a little of the whisky,' urged Mr Edward. 'It will do you good.'

I took a small, cautious sip. Though it burned, I found the whisky bracing. 'Last night I decided to head out to visit the scene of the original crime. When I was telling Merry of this I wondered if I was overheard. Last night someone also tried to break into our room.'

'Euphemia, you didn't say anything of this?' exclaimed Rory. 'You put yourself in mortal danger!'

'I cannot but agree,' said Mr Edward.

'Perhaps I was foolish to go ahead with my plan,' I said. 'But I wasn't sure I had been overheard and for all I knew whoever tried to break into our room was merely an inebriated or over-amorous guest.'

'I think you knew neither of those to be true,' said Mr Edward.

'Perhaps,' I admitted. 'But it was clear to me the situation was getting worse. There was too much unexplained and you were all too eager for Susan to take the blame. I thought if I visited the site it might help me make the mental connections necessary to come to the truth.'

'Did it?' asked Mr Edward.

I sighed. 'No, I only understood McGillvary was both the intruder and the killer when he levelled his gun at us.'

'I take it you followed Euphemia when you heard she had gone out alone?'

'It was pure chance that Merry told me. She had obviously risen straight after Euphemia and

181

was occupying herself rearranging the kitchen. I heard a crash...'

I was filled with foreboding. 'Not the dish with the green leaves on the lid?' I asked.

'I'm afraid so,' said Rory. 'She was in a terrible state of worry about you. So I decided to set out at once. How you got there before me...'

'I got a lift.'

'With whom?' asked Mr Edward.

'Donal Strachan, the gamekeeper.'

Mr Edward flicked open a notebook and wrote down the name. 'I shall have a quiet word with Mr Strachan. I think a romantic tryst between the two of you is the best excuse.'

'But there's been a murder done,' said Rory. 'He was saving us, but Fitzroy shot McGillvary.'

'I never spotted him,' said Mr Edward sadly. 'But Fitzroy has been shadowing him for the last two days. He was convinced and his instincts are usually correct. Did he leave the body up there?'

Rory gawped at him.

'Yes,' I said.

'That will also have to be cleared up. I believe the drive is finished. I shall arrange for the local police to investigate.' He smiled slightly. 'I am sure I can trust them to get this wrong. A little shooting accident, I think. The gentlemen of this house are uncommonly bad with firearms.'

Rory sprung to his feet. 'What kind of a policeman are you?' he demanded.

'The kind who requires you to sign these papers.' He indicated two sheets on an occasional table. I got up and read them over. Rory raged behind me. I caught words such as 'murderer', 'truth' and 'justice', but mostly my thoughts were caught up with what I was reading.

'Rory,' I said in a low but carrying voice. 'You need to see this. These are papers in which we promise, for the sake of King and country, we will never reveal what we have seen today.'

'What?' asked Rory. He came over and read them beside me.

'It is true then,' I asked softly, 'that we are on the eve of war?'

'Not the eve. Not yet,' said Mr Edward. 'This is an extraordinary time and at these times extraordinary actions are necessary.'

'Even condoning murder?' said Rory.

'You can regard what happened to McGillvary as an execution. If all the truth had come out at his trial he would undoubtedly have been hanged.'

'That's what Fitzroy called it,' I said. 'But it's not the same as being tried by a jury of your peers, 12 good men.'

'I agree,' said Mr Edward. 'If the evidence had been presented I would have had no option but to take him to trial. Fitzroy is a different matter. He has the King's authority to do what is necessary for the security of the kingdom.' He looked at Rory. 'It might make it easier for you if you thought of him as a soldier.'

'He shot him in the back,' said Rory with obvious distaste.

'I imagine he believed it to be necessary to secure the outcome he desired.'

'He's right, Rory. If he had called to McGillvary, the man would have shot him, then you,

183

and I don't like to think what would have been my fate.'

'No, of course not,' said Rory. 'I didn't mean that, Euphemia. But this all seems so wrong.'

'You have an alarming streak of chivalry for a butler,' said Mr Edward. 'I'd accuse you of aping your betters, but I have met your house guests.'

The last piece suddenly clicked into place. Mentally, I heard Tipton telling me about Rolly. 'Rolly – Roland McGillvary,' I said. 'He suggested to Tipton that I was of easy virtue – that's how he drew you off. He knew you were too chivalrous to leave me to Tipton's advances. You owe him nothing.'

'No, I don't,' said Rory. 'But I still don't like this.'

'It really is for the best,' said Mr Edward, handing Rory a pen.

'Aye, I guess the man tried to have me hanged and then tried to kill me.' He signed.

'Euphemia?'

'I will sign. But as much because of what might happen if I did not,' I said.

'Euphemia,' said Rory. 'You can't think these gentlemen would do anything to harm us?'

'I think,' I said carefully, 'that Mr Fitzroy, at least, will do what he considers necessary.'

'Exactly,' said Mr Edward. 'Now, might I suggest you change before the rest of the household sees the state you are in? I will explain during your romantic wanderings you came upon the body of McGillvary and came straight to me.'

'I am not comfortable with this. We are damaging Euphemia's reputation.'

'I wouldn't worry,' said Mr Edward. 'I am sure Euphemia's unusual reputation can bear this.'

He ushered us out of the door. I found I could not look Rory in the face. Within the hour, the whole household would believe we had been dallying together. What I was asked to do for King and country!

I hurried to my chamber. Someone had sent up hot water and I had an impromptu standing bath in front of the bedchamber fire, which had also mysteriously been lit. It took me some while to rid my person – especially my hair – of the thick, black and foul-smelling Scottish mud. When I finally made my way downstairs, it was to hear Lord Richard bellowing in the hall. I stopped on the landing, not wishing to add to the trauma of the day by encountering him in full wrath. He was yelling at Rory.

'Damn fools! Can no one but me handle a bloody gun? That's it. It's over. One accident I can live with! But two! I'll have to sell the bloody place. Pack it up, man, we're going home! The party is over.'

'Do you believe there were two accidents?' I jumped at Mr Bertram's voice in my ear.

'What ... what else could it be?' I stammered.

'Am I to wish Mr McLeod and you happy?' asked Mr Bertram.

'What? No!' I cried. 'Certainly not.'

'Only, I hear you were keeping company together.' He had the grace to look embarrassed. 'That you were courting when you came across the grisly scene. You don't strike me as a girl who would trifle with a man's heart, Euphemia. Nor

185

as one who would go out walking, as they say, with any man.'

It was my turn to blush with embarrassment. I could not meet his gaze. 'The situation has been misunderstood, sir.'

'I hope it has,' he said.

'Do you, sir?' I said hopefully.

'Yes,' said Mr Bertram gravely. 'While we would do all in our power to assist McLeod if you and he were to marry, we cannot have the house and staff duties disrupted due to relationships between servants.'

I felt my mouth fall open. No words came out.

'Mrs Wilson wouldn't like it,' said Mr Bertram.

I pulled myself together. 'No, of course not, sir. I wouldn't want to distress Mrs Wilson.'

'I think it's best,' continued Mr Bertram frowning, 'if this story is not referred to again.'

'As you wish, sir.'

'I'm not a fool, Euphemia. I know there's more going on here than you are willing to tell me. Mr Edward spent overly long interviewing you. As you have not seen fit to let me into your confidence, I suggest that we never refer again to anything that happened over these last few days.'

'What happened in Scotland shall stay in Scotland,' I said tersely.

'Agreed,' said Mr Bertram. 'Will you speak to McLeod or shall I?'

'Oh, I think such instruction should come from the family, sir, and not a mere fellow servant.'

'There is no need for us to fall out over this,' said Mr Bertram.

'Fall out, sir? I don't understand. I'm your

186

brother's servant and I hope I give good service to all the family.'

'Damn it! You know what I mean. We have an unusual, er, relationship.'

'I hesitate to be so rude as to contradict you, sir, but as I now understand it, sir, no servants of this household are allowed relationships.'

'That isn't what I meant and you know it! There has always been something more than servant and master between us. If it wasn't so damn ridiculous, I would say we were friends.'

'As you say, sir, that is ridiculous. If you will excuse me I have duties to attend to.'

'Euphemia!'

I pretended not to hear and walked away. Mr Bertram did not follow. I was therefore in a state of considerable agitation when I came across Mr Edward in the passages leading to the kitchen.

'I was explaining to Susan that her pension will now be honoured,' he said.

'Mr Bertram?' I asked hopefully.

'No, Lord Richard has reconsidered his position concerning the management of the estate.'

'You're watching him, aren't you?'

'I couldn't say,' said Mr Edward.

'Is this because of what happened before? To his father?' I asked.

'Miss St John, can I advise you not to meddle in matters that don't concern you? You have already more cause than most to understand that sometimes the security of the nation must be put before a single act.'

'You know what he is, don't you?'

'I refer you to my previous answer.'

187

'You need him for something... The war.'

'If you pray, Miss St John, pray that whatever we need him for never happens. We will do what is necessary.'

'But you would rather it wasn't necessary,' I said.

Mr Edward smiled. 'You begin to understand. Now, I must be on my way. Fitzroy will want a full report.'

'You work for him?' I asked surprised.

'Let's just say that Mr Fitzroy is almost a law unto himself. Almost.'

'While you are being so candid, sir, could you possibly tell me why these deaths occurred.'

Mr Edward sighed. 'If I *am* being candid, it is in the hope our paths never cross again, for both our sakes. But as for explaining everything that happened, my dear girl, it would take hours. May I suggest you watch the newspaper headlines for news of the Far East in the coming days?'

I knew I had pushed him as far as he would allow me, so I put out my hand. 'Let us part friends, sir. After all we are both loyal servants of the Crown,' I said.

Mr Edward put his large hand around mine. 'You know, Euphemia, this could all have been solved much more quickly and neatly if you had talked to the person who had the other half of the puzzle you held.'

'I did talk to Mr Fitzroy! He told me he always worked alone.'

'I was referring to Mr Bertram,' said Mr Edward. He shook my hand firmly and walked away without another word.

I walked into the kitchen, my head whirling with thoughts. Merry ran up to me. 'Is it true we're to leave early?'

'I believe so,' I said.

'Thank goodness!' said Merry.

EPILOGUE

Although Merry would have been happy to leave within the hour, despite the attentions of her local swain, who so loved showing her views, it was a full day before we were on our way and many weary travelling hours later before we were back within the portals of Stapleford Hall. As the carriage trundled up the familiar drive, I experienced the curious sensation of relief. Stapleford Hall was hardly a welcoming place, but it had become, in the strangest way, my home. I might loathe and disrespect many of the Staplefords, but the people who lived and worked below stairs had become my new family and I was comfortable with them. Merry, Bobby, Willie and, of course, Rory, I counted as true friends. But like any homecoming, it was to be a mixed blessing.

I returned to find my services as housekeeper were no longer required. The determined Mrs Wilson had cajoled Miss Richenda into obtaining her a wheeled bath chair, so she could readily direct the operation of the house. Bobby quickly grew into the habit of forgetting to grease her wheels, so when we heard her squeaky approach, if necessary, we could remove ourselves to the upper part of the house. However, Rory, who remained as butler, ensured we did not often avail ourselves of this respite.

He and I remained on reasonable terms although he was now Mr McLeod to me. We didn't speak of the events up north, or of whatever Mr Bertram had said to him, but there was a distance between us at his instigation. I remained unreservedly grateful to him for saving my life and did all in my power to ensure our previous relationship did not endanger his position. In turn Rory, unasked, spoke to Lord Richard and I found myself promoted again from maid to underhousekeeper. Merry told me she had overheard Rory point out that a housekeeper, who could only oversee the ground floor of a three-storey house needed assistance. At this point, she had to run away as she heard the squeak of wheels behind her, so I do not know what other arguments Rory employed, but I was grateful to him once more.

It was around this time that Mr Bertram disappeared from the household. No one mentioned his going. We were simply told one morning to put his room into dust sheets, so it seemed unlikely he would return shortly.

Life continued a busy schedule of dusting, cleaning and sundry domestic duties. At first, it was a relief after Scotland and I think all the staff felt comfort in the return to normality. But the human heart is a fickle thing and it was not too long before I found myself sighing over the duty of darning linen. Lord Richard had shouted at me twice that day for no good reason and, as I sat in the linen room, sewing in the dim light with my incautiously large stitches, I could not help but wonder if this was to be the extent of my recklessness to the end of my days. I am ashamed to say I felt quite dismayed at the prospect.

I chided myself that I had no cause to be so downhearted. Thanks to Rory's intervention I now earned enough to ensure that Mother and Little Joe could manage quite adequately. Mother's piano lessons were becoming, she told me, most in demand. Little Joe must soon go to school and I was attempting to put aside savings for this, as I believe was Mother. Between us we would manage. I had a good position. After everything that occurred, Lord Richard treated me with, if not civility, more respect that he showed any other woman of the household. Even Miss Richenda seemed to have been brought to heel and gave me no more cause for annoyance. Mr Bertram had gone, but it was probably for the best. I was a little lonely, but Merry and I were better friends than ever before and her cheery nature often helped lift my spirits. However, I also knew it often helped lift the spirits of a local lad who wasn't, Merry assured me, one for views. I knew that one day in the not too far future, she would marry, if not this young man, then another and leave service to start her own family. I was, of course, pleased for her at this prospect, but I saw myself growing old with only Mrs Wilson for company and that was a most lowering thought. Sometimes, I fancied Rory's eyes lingered on me for longer than was necessary and with more warmth than he might be expected to show to a fellow servant, but he never by word indicated that he would so much as value a conversation alone with me and I could hardly approach him. His presence to me was a comfort and I could only hope he would come to realise this.

A tear dripped from my cheek onto the sheet I was darning. I wiped it away and gave a big sigh. Really, I had much to be grateful for. I could not wish for better.

It was at this point that the linen door burst open and admitted Mr Bertram to turn my life upside down once more.

He was brandishing a newspaper. 'Have you seen this, Euphemia! The new treaty? Japan has annexed Korea once more. That's what it was all about!'

'Sir,' I said jumping to my feet and dropping my mending all over the floor. 'I didn't expect to see you again.'

Mr Bertram began to pick up the sheets from the floor. He spoke quickly and breathlessly. 'I owe you an apology, Euphemia. My God, if you'd listened to me Rory McLeod would have been hanged. Your instincts, as ever, were right. I should have listened to you. I apologise.'

'Really, sir, there is no need,' I said. Although I felt the apology was well-deserved.

'Of course I was right about it being an international affair rather than a local one,' said Bertram.

'Indeed you were, sir,' I said, smiling.

Bertram's face broke into a grin. 'That's very gracious of you.' He placed the sheets carefully to one side. 'I wasn't at my best in the Highlands. I know that.' He swallowed. 'What you said to me ... what you said to me about staying here for the sake of this house built from blood and death...' He took a deep breath and I knew he was struggling with some deep emotions.

'I do understand, sir. Your position has been a difficult one...'

Bertram grasped my hand and spoke earnestly. 'No. No. You were right. I don't want it. I don't need to stay here. I'd fallen into... I don't know what I'd fallen into. Perhaps the hope I'd catch Richard out? I'd like to say that was it, but I think the idea of change was too different. Too difficult.' He took my other hand too. We stood there, he holding both my hands. His eyes shone with excitement. 'But I've done it, Euphemia. I've done it.' His eyes were alight. 'And I want you to come with me!'

I swallowed hard. 'Bertram,' I said. 'Can you mean? Do you mean?'

'Yes,' said Mr Bertram. 'I've bought my own home and I want you to live there.'

'Bertram!'

'Euphemia!' Mr Bertram gripped my hands more firmly in his. I looked shyly up at him

'Yes, Bertram?'

His face broke into a broad grin as he said, 'I want you to be my housekeeper!'

Yet again, it was not the declaration I had hoped for. I struggled to compose myself. Mr Bertram watched me, hopefully. This could open up a new horizon of possibilities. Anything was better than darning laundry and, away from Stapleford Hall, who knew what adventures might await me? An unwanted thought rose in my mind: if I left Stapleford Hall, would I ever see Rory McLeod again?

'Well, Euphemia? Will you do it?'

The publishers hope that this book has given you enjoyable reading. Large Print Books are especially designed to be as easy to see and hold as possible. If you wish a complete list of our books please ask at your local library or write directly to:

Magna Large Print Books
Magna House, Long Preston,
Skipton, North Yorkshire.
BD23 4ND

This Large Print Book for the partially sighted, who cannot read normal print, is published under the auspices of

THE ULVERSCROFT FOUNDATION

THE ULVERSCROFT FOUNDATION

... we hope that you have enjoyed this Large Print Book. Please think for a moment about those people who have worse eyesight problems than you ... and are unable to even read or enjoy Large Print, without great difficulty.

You can help them by sending a donation, large or small to:

**The Ulverscroft Foundation,
1, The Green, Bradgate Road,
Anstey, Leicestershire, LE7 7FU,
England.**
or request a copy of our brochure for more details.

The Foundation will use all your help to assist those people who are handicapped by various sight problems and need special attention.

Thank you very much for your help.